It's the first Christm
several new resident
the first time—or fc

lagher works to save his hometown from withering away by relocating his business empire there, the only gift he really wants is to marry the teenage sweetheart he thought he'd lost forever—but Veronica Patton Butler has other hearts to care for, however much she loves Jackson.

Bridger Calhoun is more than ready to make Penelope Gallagher his bride, but however much she adores him, Shark Girl is dragging her heels on tying the knot—which seems to be a maddening tradition among Gallagher women.

Come join the fun…the heartache…the sweetness, as Sweetgrass prepares for a community celebration that will bring the Morning Star Gallaghers and the Marshalls to town, along with several of Jackson's Seattle geeks and more than one lost soul about to find a place to belong—in eccentric, lovable, unforgettable Sweetgrass Springs…where hope never fades and love never dies.

BOOKS BY JEAN BRASHEAR

SWEETGRASS SPRINGS:
Texas Roots
Texas Wild
Texas Dreams
Texas Rebel
Texas Blaze
Texas Christmas Bride
The Book Babes
Texas Hope
Texas Strong

Texas Sweet
Be Mine This Christmas
Texas Charm
Texas Magic
Be My Midnight Kiss

THE GALLAGHERS OF MORNING STAR
(cousins of the Sweetgrass Springs clan)
Texas Secrets
Texas Lonely
Texas Bad Boy

LONE STAR LOVERS
Texas Heartthrob
Texas Healer
Texas Protector
Texas Deception
Texas Lost
Texas Wanderer
Texas Bodyguard
Texas Rescue

THE MARSHALLS
Texas Refuge
Texas Star
Texas Danger

THE GODDESS OF FRIED OKRA

SECOND CHANCES series
Guarding Gaby
Bringing Bella Back
The Price He Paid
The House That Love Built
The Road Back Home
Dream House

DANGEROUS TO LOVE collection
The Light Walker
The Choice
Mercy

Texas Christmas Bride

Bride

Sweetgrass Springs
Book Six

Jean Brashear

Dedication

To my fellow Handcrafts Unlimited volunteer quilters: Joyce Walden, Earlene Dorsa, Ruth Sudduth, Linda Vise, Jane Shurtleff, Ceci Sinnwell, Mel Brown and Linda Johnson, as well as the Thursday afternoon shop volunteers Pat, Florence, Martha and Marilyn. Thanks for welcoming me into the fold and for swapping stories, sharing quilting wisdom and generally indulging in all kinds of foolishness with me. I do love our Thursday afternoon therapy sessions!

And, as always, to Ercel, who has embraced this pie-in-the-sky romantic's wild notions with open arms and keeps my faith in love burning bright.

Acknowledgments

With my deepest gratitude all you lovely readers who keep asking for more Sweetgrass stories—and special thanks to Teresa Maksim, who thought we needed a Christmas story. You were absolutely right, and I thank you for the encouragement that made me go back and try one…more…time. Hope you like the results!

For all the gang on my Facebook author page, thanks for the fun and the very helpful discussion about what Ben should call Jackson. You really helped me stop overthinking!

I very much appreciate the help from my favorite flower farmer, Pamela Arnosky, who came to my rescue this time to figure out what Veronica would have available for wedding flowers in December.

Big thanks to Jackie Paris for the last-minute read— any errors left are on me!

I'm especially grateful to Nancy Smith Munger, my own cherished childhood friend, for many reasons—but right now, I can't thank her enough for being a godsend in helping me keep this ever-expanding cast of characters straight!

PS Please note the cookie recipes to be found at the end of this book, contributed by my quilter friends (you'll see them in guest appearances in this book.) I haven't made them all yet, but they look so yummy I intend to!

The Families of Sweetgrass Springs

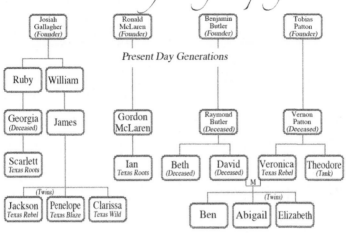

Present Day Generations

The Gallaghers

Present Day Descendants of Josiah Gallagher

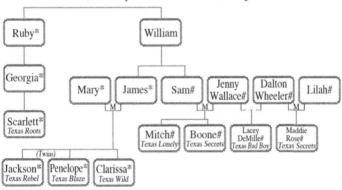

[M] = Married
[_ _ _] = Affair
* = Gallaghers of Sweetgrass Springs
# = Gallaghers of Morning Star

SWEETGRASS SPRINGS

Cast of Characters

(titles in parentheses mark a character's primary story)

THE FOUR FOUNDING FAMILIES:

THE GALLAGHERS

(Josiah Gallagher, Sweetgrass Springs founder)

Ruby Gallagher – diner owner and the heart and soul of this struggling small town

James Gallagher – Ruby's brother and father of twins Jackson and Penny plus Rissa.

Scarlett Ross – Ruby's granddaughter, New York chef whose deceased mother Georgia never told her they had family in Texas (*Texas Roots, Texas Dreams*)

Jackson Gallagher – video game tycoon and prodigal son of James who's been missing for twenty years (*Texas Rebel, Texas Christmas Bride*)

Penelope Gallagher – Jackson's twin sister, shark lawyer who left Sweetgrass Springs behind (*Texas Blaze, Texas Christmas Bride*)

Clarissa Gallagher – youngest child of James and horse whisperer; the only one of James's children who cares about the ranch (*Texas Wild*)

THE MCLARENS

(Ronald McLaren, Sweetgrass Springs founder)

Gordon McLaren – owner of the Double Bar M Ranch with his son Ian (*Texas Hope*)

Ian McLaren – Gordon's son whose mother abandoned him as a child; now runs Double Bar M Ranch. Unofficial mayor of Sweetgrass Springs and its mainstay alongside Ruby (*Texas Roots,*

Texas Dreams)

Sophia McLaren Cavanaugh – the mother Ian has never forgiven for leaving him behind (*Texas Hope*)

Michael Cavanaugh – Ian's half-brother by Sophia's second husband. Neither Michael nor Ian was ever told the other exists (*The Book Babes, Texas Hope*)

THE PATTONS
(Tobias Patton, Sweetgrass Springs founder)

Vernon Patton – deceased, abusive father of Veronica and Theodore (Tank)

Veronica Patton Butler – Jackson Gallagher's teenage sweetheart left behind when he vanished. She married Jackson's close friend David Butler. Owner of a flower farm and David's widow (*Texas Rebel, Texas Christmas Bride*)

Theodore "Tank" Patton – deputy sheriff and the most reviled man in Sweetgrass Springs (*Texas Hope*)

THE BUTLERS
(Benjamin Butler, Sweetgrass Springs founder)

Raymond Butler – deceased father of David Butler

David Butler – one of the most beloved citizens of Sweetgrass Springs. High school buddies with Jackson Gallagher, Ian McLaren and Randall Mackey. Died leaving his widow Veronica with a son Ben and twins Abby and Beth.

Beth Butler – David's sister who died in the car accident that caused Jackson Gallagher to be banished

OTHER IMPORTANT
SWEETGRASS SPRINGS CHARACTERS:

Randall Mackey, close friend of Ian McLaren, Jackson Gallagher and David Butler. Joined the Navy after high school; became a SEAL. After leaving the service, wound up as a stuntman in Hollywood (*Texas Wild*)

Bridger Calhoun, former SEAL buddy of Mackey's, now a firefighter (*Texas Blaze, Texas Christmas Bride*)

Harley Sykes (wife Melba, a quilter) – one of the coffee group that meets every morning at Ruby's. One of the town's most colorful characters.

Raymond Benefield (wife Nita, also a quilter) – one of the coffee group regulars.

Arnie Howard – coffee group regular at Ruby's who's been warming Ruby's bed for many years but can never convince her to marry him

Jeanette Carson – sharp-tongued veteran waitress at Ruby's. Attended high school a few years behind Ian McLaren, for whom she's been carrying a torch for years (*Texas Charm*)

Brenda Jones – skittish teenaged waitress at Ruby's who just showed up in Sweetgrass one day and has secrets she keeps (*Texas Sweet*)

Henry Jansen – busboy turned cook at Ruby's; young man whose chivalry towards Brenda turns to blushes when noticed (*Texas Sweet*)

Spike Ridley – tattooed Goth pastry chef with an attitude; her skills are unparalleled, but her motto might as well be "have mixer will travel."

Walker Roundtree – country music superstar; spars with Jeanette and performs at several Sweetgrass weddings (*Texas Charm*)

EXPLORE

Sweetgrass Springs

BEFORE

1. Building
2. Vacant Lot
3. Storefront
4. Ruby's Diner
5. Storefront
6. Storefront
7. Ruby Gallagher's Boarding House
8. Vacant Lot
9. House
10. Raymond and Nita Benefield's House
11. Jeanette Carson's House
12. Harley and Melba Sykes House
13. Mickan's Garage
14. Storefront
15. Storefront
16. House
17. Arnie Howard's House

The Legend of Sweetgrass Springs

L ost and alone and dying, thirsty and days without food, the wounded soldier fell from his half-dead horse only yards from life-giving water. His horse nickered at the scent, and the soldier gathered one last effort to belly his way to the edge of the spring.

But there he faltered. Bleeding from shoulder and thigh, he felt the darkness close in on him and sorrowed for his men, for the battle he would lose, for the fight he would not finish. In his last seconds of life, he wished for the love he would never find.

Rest, a lovely, musical voice said.

He managed to drag his eyes open once more.

And gazed upon the face of the most beautiful woman he'd ever seen.

And perhaps the saddest. Her eyes were midnight blue and filled with a terrible grief as she lifted a hand toward him.

I am dying, he thought. *I will never know her.*

But the woman smiled and tenderly caressed his face

as she cradled his head and brought life-giving water to his lips.

You will live, she said. *Be at peace. Let the spring heal you.*

Around him the air went soft, the water slid down his throat like a blessing. His battered body relaxed, and the pain receded.

Sleep, she said. *I will watch over you.*

He complied, his eyes heavy. His injuries were too severe; he knew he could not live. But though he would not wake up, he was one of the fortunate, to have an angel escort him into the afterlife. *Thank you*, he managed with his last breath.

Wake. All is well.

The soldier opened his eyes, surprised to feel soft grass beneath him, trees whispering overhead. From nearby, he heard the bubbling music of the spring.

Then he saw her, his angel. *Where am I? Is this heaven?*

Her lips curved, but her eyes were again midnight dark with sorrow. *You are still of this world.*

Who are you? he asked. *Why are you sad?*

She searched his eyes. *Will you stay with me?*

I would like nothing more, but I cannot. I must return to my men.

She turned her face away, and he felt her grief as his own.

I'll come back. When the battle is over and I am done, I will come back to you.

You won't. A terrible acceptance filled her gaze. *I will never have love. Once I was mortal like you, and I was loved, but I turned away from it. From him, my one true love. He was beloved of The Fates, and they cursed me to wait. I cannot leave this place.*

Wait for what?

It doesn't matter, she said sadly. *You must go. They always go.*

I'll come back. I'll set you free. Tell me how, and I'll do it.

She stared into him for a long time, then shook her head. *There's only one way.*

What is it? he asked eagerly, rising strong and well again, already searching for his horse to ride away.

She watched him in silence. Made herself invisible because she knew.

Where did you go? he called out, searching the clearing, striding to the spring to peer into its depths. When he didn't see her, with a heavy heart he mounted, but for a moment he lingered. *I'll come back, I promise. You can tell me then. I'm sorry, but my men need me, and I have to go. I will return for you.*

He wouldn't, she knew. They never did. She'd brought her eternal loneliness on herself, and she was losing hope.

So she watched him ride away after one last look.

Only love can set me free, she whispered softly.

Love strong enough to stay.

Chapter One

"Why did I think it was a good idea to cater Jackson's company Christmas party with Nana off on her honeymoon?" Scarlett McLaren moaned as she juggled pans in the kitchen of her grandmother's diner.

"Because pregnancy hormones have fried your brain?" answered veteran waitress Jeanette Carson.

Sweetgrass Springs was so small that they were all doing double-duty until Scarlett could properly staff Ruby's Dream. The high-end restaurant and events center was her brainchild, created from the old decommissioned courthouse her grandmother Ruby had held onto for years, hoping to someday make Sweetgrass thrive once more. Juggling the need to keep her grandmother's diner open while searching fruitlessly for restaurant talent who'd relocate to this tiny burg, Scarlett was a good month behind her planned schedule for opening the new place.

She'd sure forgotten to plug getting pregnant into her schedule.

But she'd promised Nana, and she was determined she'd make Sweetgrass vibrant again.

"A misguided sense of love, City Girl," opined Scarlett's cousin, Rissa Gallagher Mackey. "My brother knows talent. He also knows a sucker when he sees one. It's how he became a bazillionaire. Go sit down for a minute."

Rissa reached for a pan, and Scarlett slapped her hand. "Don't even think about it," she growled.

"Hey, I can cook. Penny's not the only one in the family."

Behind them, Rissa's hot husband snickered. "Babe, step away from the stove." Randall Mackey smiled and drew her into his arms. "No offense, darlin'. Everyone knows you're a genius with horses. We all have our strengths. Plus some of us multi-task." Mackey nodded toward Rissa's sister Penny, cooking with a bluetooth in her ear, talking a mile a minute. "Anybody know who she's talking to?"

"China, probably. Or Katmandu—who knows? Poor Bridger. Ever since she took the job helping Jackson run his video game empire, I don't think her phone has left her side. It's probably surgically attached," Rissa mused.

"You didn't catch the two of them making out at the spring last night, obviously." Mackey grinned. "My man has his talents, and one of them is seducing Shark Girl right out of her socks." He peered around Rissa. "Is she cooking in…stilettos? Doesn't that hurt?"

Just then, a young voice piped up from the doorway to the dining room. "Cousin Scarlett, could we do it again, the Gallagher Thanksgiving meal? Where everybody is there?" Rissa and Mackey's adopted son Eric asked.

"Absolutely. Every Thanksgiving. Consider it a standing date."

The seven-year-old didn't look reassured. He opened his mouth, then shut it.

"What is it?"

His eyes slid to the side. "For Christmas, I meant," he said softly. "Only maybe...better." The child had come a long way from the abuse of his past, but he was still hesitant to ask for much. "Never mind."

"What do you mean by better? What would you like us to do differently?"

Eric pointed around the room. "Them."

"Them? Oh, you mean invite more people?"

Blonde hair bounced as he nodded eagerly. "Some people don't have anybody. They shouldn't be sad on Christmas Day."

"I can't argue with that."

Rissa's gaze met hers, dark with anguish over what this child had suffered in his short life. "We're going to have a great Christmas, Eric. I promise you that."

Perfect trust showed in the boy's face as he looked up at his new mother. "I know that. But I want everyone to have one."

"Let me think on it, Eric," Scarlett responded. And tried not to feel exhausted. Christmas. Lordy, she'd barely survived Thanksgiving. She'd loved having everyone together, but brutal morning sickness seemed as though it would never end. She'd shoved Nana off on her extended honeymoon right after, lying through her teeth that she felt fine. Her husband Ian was still being a bear because he knew the truth, hovering over her every move like an avenging angel.

She noticed their second waitress, Brenda Jones, avidly listening. The girl was a mystery to them all, a stray, probably a runaway, sweet and shy and nervous. Nana had taken her in, no questions asked.

"What did you all do for Christmas back home, Brenda?"

The timid girl halted mid-step. "Me?"

Scarlett nodded for her to continue.

Hazel eyes darted like a frantic rabbit. "Nothing special." Brenda's slight shoulders curled inward.

Shy former busboy turned cook's helper Henry Jansen, of all people, piped up to cover the awkwardness. "My granny worked for other folks a lot, so we saved our celebrating until Christmas night, after she was done serving the rich folks." His chin remained high, his expression forbidding pity. "Soon as I was old enough, I helped her whenever I was allowed. We got to take the leftovers home, and I knew Granny liked that because she could get off her feet and skip cooking a meal. I learned to cook soon as I got big enough. Not like you, of course."

"You're turning into a fine cook now, Henry." Scarlett glanced between the two, then wondered who else here had experienced a less than storybook Christmas. Here she'd thought she was the only one who'd passed that holiday and so many more longing for what she was sure everyone else had. Mama had tried hard to make the day special, but with no family around…

Her heart clenched as she thought about how much family she'd had here, all along. She and her mother hadn't needed to be alone.

She'd never understand how a mother could rob her own child of that. She stroked her belly and made a promise. *You will never be so terribly alone.*

Meanwhile, there were people here whose pasts she couldn't change.

But their present day could be very different. "Eric," she called out.

"Yes, ma'am?"

Scarlett caught Rissa's beaming pride at her adopted son's manners.

"Tell me more about what better looks like to you."

"Really?" Hope bloomed on the child's face.

"Really."

The boy thought for a minute. "It was pretty great when everyone was here for the surprise weddings. Could we invite Dalton and Sam's family and Emilio and Antonio's family and all of the others who were here?" In other words, not only the whole town, but also the Morning Star Gallaghers and the Marshall clan.

"Honey, they might already have other plans," Rissa began.

"But they might not, right?"

Scarlett laughed. "The only way to find out is to ask."

"Seriously?"

"Seriously." Even if she couldn't seem to get a restaurant open, surely she could do this. Her horrific morning sickness had finally begun to ease.

"Scarlett..." Rissa warned. "You are just barely holding on. Don't even think about it."

Wow. If Cousin Crankypants, who'd loathed her the

moment she'd set foot in town, was worrying over her...

"I'm telling Ian," Penny spoke up, off the phone at last. "This is not a good idea."

"I think it's a splendid idea," Scarlett insisted. She'd seen Brenda's eyes light with hope and Henry smile as he chopped vegetables. *Later*, she mouthed to Rissa and to Penny, who shook her head impatiently.

"So I'm thinking that maybe we put up a big tree in the courthouse and another one out on the lawn. We can serve over there and use the upstairs if we need it. Everyone can bring card tables and chairs. With the upgraded kitchen, there's more room to cook."

"If you're going to be crazy enough to volunteer for that, Scarlett, it has to be a community effort." Melba Sykes stepped around the kitchen door, eavesdropping as usual. Melba considered gossip a noble pursuit and her God-given duty. "We'll do it like a church social. You are not cooking for this whole town."

"Bridger can barbecue," Penny offered.

"Barbecue's not Christmas dinner food," Scarlett protested.

"It is in Texas. Any day is a good one for barbecue, am I right?" Rissa scanned the room.

Heads nodded.

"We're not in Merry Old England. Or Bedford Falls," Rissa pointed out. "Jimmy Stewart doesn't live here."

"But he'd want barbecue if he did," Harley Sykes shouted.

There was laughter and a smattering of applause.

Melba spoke up. "Josh Marshall would bring a whole

new flair to George Bailey."

"Especially if he performed the role with his shirt off," piped up Earlene Dorsa, another of the quilting group.

A couple of whistles amid more laughter.

"Everybody brings a dish. That's the way it's done. Surely you've been in Sweetgrass long enough to know that. Just because you're a Paris-trained chef and the best cook in the state doesn't mean you're the only one," quilter Joyce Walden insisted. "We'll get a signup list going, so we can plan. Can we bring family if we have relatives coming in?"

Scarlett didn't have to think twice to answer. "Of course. Goes without saying."

"Anyone who can't get out, we'll either pick them up or take them a plate," suggested Ruth Sudduth.

"And we can set up a secret Santa so all the kids get a gift," proposed Rissa.

Because not all of them would, otherwise, Scarlett realized, glancing at Eric and wondering what his Christmases had been like with only a mother who had had a penchant for abusive men. Eric would be inundated with gifts from his new family, she knew.

But there were other Erics.

She turned to look at Brenda and wondered. Made a mental note to make sure the diner staff got presents, too.

She thought about her cousin Jackson, Rissa and Penny's brother, who'd been away from home for so long. Had he celebrated at all? Based on what she knew, she doubted it. The fact that he was immensely wealthy couldn't make up for being essentially alone.

His Christmas this year would be so much better, she was certain. He needed family as much as she did. As Brenda and Henry and Jeanette and Bridger did…

"You're a genius, Eric," she called out. The boy's face went bright with joy and hope. "It's gonna be a great Christmas. Thank you."

The child's smile could barely be contained in those round cheeks. He'd lost the gaunt look he'd had when she first met him.

"Ian is going to have a cow," Rissa muttered.

"He already owns a whole herd of them," Scarlett reminded her. "Now if Santa would just bring me a pastry chef, I promise to be a good girl all year."

"That's gonna happen." Rissa rolled her eyes.

Headed over to one of the abandoned downtown buildings to meet his future brother-in-law Jackson, Bridger Calhoun could barely recall Christmas with his family. He wondered if his newly-found sister Molly remembered anything at all beyond screaming and tension. He'd have to ask her when she came for the holiday.

After he'd gone into the service, Christmas was mostly firefights or boredom on the base, augmented by the occasional care packages from strangers. Not that those weren't appreciated—they were. But sometimes kindness was harder to take than closing yourself off.

Pretending holidays were just another day.

This Christmas, however, would be one for the books. He'd worked a deal with Penelope's dad and Rissa and Jackson, carving out a spot on Gallagher land that he'd wanted to buy for a home for the two of them, but her dad insisted that he intended to deed it to them as a wedding gift.

Bridger would damn well pay for the house himself, though. Legs might have buckets more money than him after selling her partnership in that pricey D.C. law firm, and she'd likely not understand why he was not going to use it, but providing for his family was important to him. He wanted to be the one to put the roof over their heads, one he and Penelope and, God willing, their children would sleep under at night.

In peace and safety.

He was determined to have the spot staked out and the foundation poured by Christmas—assuming he could ever get her to stop tweaking the plans, that is. She might not have the Suzy Homemaker gene, but you'd never know it from the intense involvement in the size and arrangement of rooms.

She wanted a big country kitchen, too. Even if she would be striding around in stilettos and on her phone every minute.

A pistol, was his Shark Girl. A force of nature.

He loved her like crazy.

Now he just had to get her to slow down long enough to get married—a problem with Gallagher women, apparently. Only his buddy Mackey had escaped, and that, Bridger admitted, was likely only because they couldn't have adopted Eric unless he and Rissa were legally a couple. But Ruby and Scarlett had both been dragged kicking and screaming, even to marry men they loved.

Penelope was following in their footsteps, best he could tell.

He had a plan or two in mind, however. Not for him Ian's patience, damn sure not Arnie Howard's willingness to ask Ruby and be refused again and again...for eighteen long years.

He wanted his woman hogtied and bound before year's end. If that made him a Neanderthal, well...

Shark Girl could just deal with it.

Jackson and Bridger glanced around the old building, one of the many vacant ones on the square. "I think it's basically sound. A lot of elbow grease needed, but once it's cleaned up, we can surely divide it into studio spaces, don't you think?"

"Still a lot of work," Bridger observed. "And you don't even know if any of your employees will agree to relocate."

"True. But I'd like to lure them here. If only there was a hotel or motel within fifty miles," Jackson sighed. "Hmm...you suppose we could get this set up for some sort of dormitory living right off, then modify later?"

"What are you thinking?"

"Scarlett's offered to cater a company event, but

housing is an issue. If they stay in Austin or San Antonio, they'll never get what's great about Sweetgrass."

"They probably won't, anyway," Bridger cautioned.

"That very well may be, but Austin's full of game professionals I can hire, if not." He smirked. "Won't mind a bit taking some designers and programmers out of Dynamo or Magstar's stables. I've already got my eye on a couple."

"Sweetgrass isn't Austin. What's in it for them here? Not everyone will appreciate what we love about it. Especially not the young guys."

"True. But much of the work can be done remotely, now that the cell tower is going up. I just—" Jackson exhaled. "I'd like to have some of them around. There's something about the synergy that results when creative people get together. Things happen that you can't plan for or predict. Humans are still hardwired to relate on levels no teleconference can replicate. We're at our best when we can see minute changes in facial features."

"Yeah. But you can get past that once you're a solid team. We had to operate on hand signals in the SEAL Teams, and that was with lives on the line."

Jackson studied him. "Ever think about teaching team building?"

"What? No. Me?"

"Penny's not the only one I had designs on, you know. I'd hire you in a heartbeat."

"I barely even play video games."

"It's your people skills I could use, Bridger. You're a leader, but one who makes people want to follow, not a dictator. You have an air of command about you, but you're not a hardass."

"I can be." Bridger scowled. "Anyway, I'm building a fire department right now. And playing medic every blasted time I turn around."

"You're a healer, through and through. A protector. People feel safe with you around."

Bridger was shaking his head.

Jackson made the kind of snap decision that had made him wealthy. "Give me two weeks of your time, whenever you can spare it."

"To do what? I don't want to work for anybody. I've taken all the orders I plan to."

Jackson snickered. "And you're marrying my twin? Hello? Have you met Penny?"

Bridger grinned. "I have Shark Girl right where I want her."

Jackson resisted rolling his eyes. Bridger was on his own there.

But he did think about the position he'd be putting Bridger in. Penny, as his second in command, would have authority over everyone but Jackson. Bridger was a strong personality, too, but that dynamic wasn't what their relationship needed. "Let me hire you as a consultant."

"I'm not traveling. I've done too much of that."

"You don't have to. I'll bring the people here. You just spend time with all of us, and I want to hear your observations. A blank slate. A fresh set of eyes."

"On what? I told you I don't know much about games."

Jackson snorted. "You know everything about gaming. You did strategic planning in life-or-death situations. You've lived the stakes that other people only try to emulate in cyberspace. I want that brain. I want your insights and reactions. Your strategic thinking plus your people skills…total win/win for me."

"I don't have that much spare time, not with building our house."

"I'll hire laborers for you."

"Nope. Non-negotiable. I'm building our house with my own hands as much as possible. I know you're crazy rich and you want the best for your sister, but…" Bridger's jaw clenched. "My children are going to live under a roof I constructed. Sleep inside a place I made safe for them."

He wasn't going to win this one, Jackson could tell. He could buy a lot of things, but not this one. "Okay, how about this? I'll trade you, labor for labor."

"What kind of labor?"

"Your choice. For every hour you spend in my world, I'll buckle on a tool belt and give you an hour on your house."

"Maybe I'd rather have your money for the fire department. There's next to no equipment."

"I was already going to do that. I have my own family to keep safe, and whatever I can do to help you build up either healthcare or fire safety, it's yours."

"You really do have an obscene amount of money, don't you?"

"I can't think of a better use for it. I don't need that much, now that I have Veronica and my children." The twins, Abby and Beth, might not be his biological issue, but they were his, regardless, just as much as Ben, the son he'd only recently come to know, the child he and Veronica had created, unbeknownst to him, before he'd disappeared.

And missed so damn much.

Bridger studied him. "Well, it's your money and your time, though I can't see that you're exactly spilling over with extra time."

"I'd like to bring Ben with me to help, if I could," Jackson made his own admission. "We're okay in Veronica's house for now, but I'd like to build us a new place once we're a little more settled in. I'd want him to help, and he's already a good hand. Hell, Bridger, the whole community would pitch in, you know they would. That's how Sweetgrass rolls. You didn't just find yourself a woman…you found a family. A whole town, related or not."

Bridger shook his head in amazement. "I never thought it could happen for me, however much I wished it would." Then he rescued them both from the uncomfortable level of emotion, wheeling to point to the far wall. "So I'm thinking we could make four studios up here, and if you wanted to drain that wallet a little more and buy the building next door, I'm pretty sure we could open that wall to connect them. Then you could have your headquarters downstairs, along with a commissary of sorts."

"I don't think Aunt Ruby would appreciate the competition."

"But Ruby's not open all night, and your geeks work all hours, right?"

"They do. Okay, I get your point. Maybe we could stock it with food from the diner, if they want the business. Scarlett's talked about catering year-round, not just this one event."

"Scarlett's taken too much on those slender shoulders, don't you think?"

"Ian sure does." Jackson sighed. "I finally got them to let me invest in Ruby's Dream and the events center, but I wish she'd let me hire her some help."

"This town is just chock full of stubborn women." Bridger grinned. "But I have to admit that any woman who can get Legs cooking while she's conference-calling to China is a force to reckon with."

They exchanged grins.

"I think I have enough to draw this up. Let's go get our women." He clapped Bridger on the shoulder, and they started down the old wooden stairs.

The second Jackson parked in the driveway, Abby burst out the door.

"Prince Daddy! I thought you'd never get home!" She raced toward his open arms and leaped in perfect trust.

He caught her, still amazed and grateful.

Home. He had only existed for too long, however many residences he owned, whatever his personal fortune. Wherever Veronica was, wherever these children were, that was now home.

A more powerful word he could not imagine.

Abby pressed her small hands on either side of his face. "What took you so long? You were gone forever!"

He couldn't help smiling. "I got back from Seattle last night, but your mom let me sleep in. I looked in on you, though. Gave you a prince kiss."

The pint-sized blonde princess had declared that he, known by her initially as Prince because she said he resembled a fairytale one, was giving her a prince kiss when he touched his lips to her forehead. She insisted on one every night before she would go to sleep.

Along with a glass of water, another story, a trip to the bathroom where she could dawdle forever doing God knows, then a second straightening of sheets and blankets and a smoothing of her pillow.

"I didn't feel it."

"Must have been because you were dreaming of…?" He cocked an eyebrow and waited. Abby's dreams were vivid and generally involved some sort of adventure. She loved detailing every second.

She screwed up her forehead. "I think…" Her brown eyes popped wide. "I know! It was about Santa! We went to Hogwarts and we had a comm—commooty Christmas with Dumbledore and Professor McGonagle and—"

"Commooty Christmas?" he asked as he carried her toward the side door.

"Uh-huh. For everybody in the whole town. And Grant and Lilah Rose and everybody!"

He stifled a laugh and started to ask more, but as he pulled the screen open, inside stood Beth, her more reserved twin. Jackson dropped to a crouch, still holding Abby. "Hey, pretty girl. How was your day?" He reached for Beth's hand but as always, left the choice to her about how to respond. Beth took her time, thought about things where Abby flung herself headlong into any given situation.

Generally chattering a mile a minute.

Beth's small hand slid into his, and her fingers curled around his far bigger ones.

Jackson's heart tumbled at her feet.

"It was fine."

"It was great, Prince Daddy!" Abby spoke over her. "Aaron Coleman threw up on the bus!"

Jackson grinned at Beth. "Did you think that was great?"

Beth's eyes sparkled, and she shook her head. "It was yuck."

"I didn't mean the throw-up was great, but then everybody started squealing and trying to get out of their seats and the bus driver yelled that we had to sit down and then he had to—"

"Abby, take a breath, honey." The love of his life appeared before him. "Hi, Jackson."

He took the opportunity to scan Veronica's slender frame from the beautiful legs he knew were hiding beneath those jeans, up over the trim waist and the sweet, soft breasts he would so like to—

"Stop that." Her cheeks were pink as he rose to his full height, a foot above hers.

"Excuse me, girls, but I need to kiss your mama now." He set Abby on her feet with a kiss to the cheek and stroked Beth's hair before he reached for the woman he'd loved since he was sixteen.

The woman he'd left behind for more years than that. "Hey, gorgeous." He reeled her in, loving the way she came to him so willingly at last.

Too much had come between them, not the least his own stupid choices. He'd never forgotten her, but he'd long ago given up on being the recipient of her love.

Then he'd seen her again and known that though everything had changed for both of them, including her marriage and widowhood and his rocky start and determined climb—

Nothing had changed, not about his feelings for her. He'd never loved another woman and never would.

"You're my everything, you know that?" he murmured before taking her lips in a slow, delicious kiss.

She sighed and softened against him. "I might have heard something about that."

"Run away with me to South America." He pressed his lips to the spot just beneath her ear that never failed to make her shiver. "We'll make love day and night."

Her sigh was soft and sweet, her body warm and welcoming to his. "Too bad supper's nearly ready."

He chuckled and rested his head against hers, eyes closed. "You're all I think about. You're—"

"Get a room, you two," snickered their sixteen-year-old Ben. "Sheesh. There are children present."

Jackson groaned, squeezed her once more, then turned to face the son he hadn't known existed until recently. Ben looked so much like him, it was like looking in a mirror at that age. His hair was Jackson's black, though he had Veronica's hazel eyes, and he possessed the same rangy build, the promise of reaching Jackson's six foot five. Jackson had no idea how people in Sweetgrass hadn't realized Ben was his son and not his buddy David's, who had married Veronica and fathered the twins. "Deal-breaker, dude. I'm gonna kiss your mom every time she needs it."

"Which is about all the time, you seem to think." But Ben's eyes were twinkling. They'd had a rough road, both of them, getting over the shock of learning Ben's true parentage. Ben had adored the man he'd thought was his father, and he'd been furious with Veronica for keeping his birth father's identity secret. Jackson had been equally furious, though he could now acknowledge what an impossible situation she'd been left in.

But they'd made a lot of progress. It had only taken a family crisis and the near-destruction of Jackson's video game company to get there.

"Hey, it's a tough job, but I'll persevere."

Ben cracked up. "So what's for dinner? I'm starving. Can I have a snack first?" Ben's near-genius IQ, rivaling Jackson's own, hadn't stopped him from playing every sport, a natural athlete as Jackson had been. That, added to the normal demands of a growing teenage male body, created the phenomenal number of calories Ben burned in a day's time.

"I have no idea how my mom did it."

Veronica leaned against him and squeezed, then left his side. "Keeping you fed, you mean? I'm surprised she didn't just throw raw steaks at you."

"Ew!" Abby cried. "That's yucky."

"Not literally, honey. Now wash your hands, and you and Bethie set the table, all right?"

"Yes, Mommy." Abby skipped from the room. Beth started after her, but turned back to Jackson.

He crouched again to be closer to her level. "What is it?"

Beth simply threw her arms around Jackson's neck and hugged him. "I'm glad you're back. I wish you could stay always."

Jackson enfolded her in his arms and rocked her slightly. "I wish I never had to go anywhere, either. I'm trying to fix things so I travel as little as possible because I miss you, too, when I'm gone." He leaned back and looked into her eyes, understanding that losing one father had hit hard at her sense of security. "I'm really careful while I'm gone." He smiled. "But I always want to tell the plane to go faster when I'm headed home. You okay, sweetie?"

"Uh-huh."

He squeezed her again. "I'd better let you get to setting the table before Ben starts eating the silverware or something."

She giggled and released him. "You're funny, Prince Daddy."

His throat too full for speech, he stroked a finger down her nose, then kissed it. She skipped after her twin.

Daddy.

A year ago—hell, a few months ago, he could never have imagined his life would hold all this. He might have possessed a boatload of money before, but now he was truly rich. Wealthy in the love Veronica had shared with him, from her own heart and in the form of her children.

Jackson rose and looked around him at the humble ranch house in which his childhood friend had sheltered this family.

Part of him envied David every last second he'd had here with them.

A larger part was profoundly grateful. And sad that for Jackson to have this bounty, David had had to leave this world.

"You all right, Dad?" Ben asked, pausing in the middle of the kitchen.

Dad. Jackson nodded, heart overflowing. "Never better, son." He summoned a smile. "So how was practice? What do you think your chances are Friday night?" He brushed a hand over Veronica's hair as he passed her and started getting out glasses to fill them with milk or iced tea.

It was all so precious. So fragile.

He was the luckiest man in the world to have gotten a second chance.

As ordered, Veronica sat watching Jackson clean up the kitchen after the meal while she drank a cup of tea. "Something's bothering you. What is it?"

"Nothing. Just business."

"You've listened to me chatter on endlessly about flower farm business, riveting details like how my poinsettia sales are going and what seeds I've started.

Now spill."

He stopped washing dishes and stared out the window over the sink. "It's Steph." He looked over his shoulder at her. "She's a mess. I have Penny now and I don't need Steph's help the way I did, but—" He shrugged. "We built Enigma Games together, the three of us: her, Ty and me. Ty's gone, and I don't feel right just putting her out to pasture, no matter how generous the severance package. But I don't know exactly what she's capable of anymore. She's not ready to work, but she's so…lost. So shaky."

"Anyone would be, after being held hostage, then watching Ty kill himself right in front of her. I can't imagine the nightmares. Bad enough you had to see the aftermath, but she wound up covered in his blood."

He drained the sink and rinsed it, then turned to face her, wiping his hands dry. "Part of me wants to just sell the whole company. Stay here in Sweetgrass. I have plenty of standing offers, and I've got more money than we'll need for the rest of our lives."

"And do what? Be my farmhand?"

"Is the position of love slave open?"

"Only to you." She rose and approached him. "Jackson, that brain of yours would never let you rest. It's been running full-tilt all your life." She combed two fingers through the unruly locks spilling over his forehead. His head bent, his shoulders sagging a little. "You're worn out."

"I'll be fine." He straightened to his full height.

"You've been through an emotional marathon. Coming back here, finding out Ben's your son, dealing with the father who banished you and left you penniless and homeless, having your best friend try to sabotage your company…to say nothing of how everyone relies on you so much while you try to pick up the pieces…it's a lot, Jackson. Too much to expect of one man."

"It's my company. They're my people." He drew her into his chest. "But you're my family."

She slid her arms around his waist. "You've got some mighty fine muscle on you. You make a decent farmhand. Not so good at taking orders, though."

He chuckled and rested his cheek on her hair.

"What if you slowed things down?" she asked. "Didn't try to move the company here for a while?"

He stiffened. "Sweetgrass is counting on me."

"Sweetgrass seems to survive, regardless. You don't have to save it singlehandedly. Scarlett and Ian are already trying to do that. I'm worried about Scarlett."

"She said she'd cater my company Christmas party if I wanted. It would be a great way to introduce my staff to Sweetgrass. Make them want to come here."

"What if you didn't do that just yet?"

"Why not?"

"Scarlett's asking too much of herself, and so are you. Take it down a notch. What if you picked several key people and brought them to Sweetgrass instead? Have you heard about the community Christmas?"

He chuckled. "You mean the commooty Christmas?"

She giggled. "Of course."

"Where did that idea come from?"

"Eric."

"Eric? Rissa's Eric?"

"Our Eric. He's a Gallagher now—well, a Mackey, technically, but—"

"Yeah. I got it. So what's up with that?"

"Everyone—and I do mean everyone, including the Morning Star branch and the Marshall clan—will be invited. Locals can bring guests."

"Wow."

"Yeah."

"Don't tell me—Scarlett plans to cook for it."

"She was going to, but that got nipped in the bud. The event has morphed into a giant pot-luck. Tree on the courthouse lawn, Secret Santa so everyone has a gift…"

He smiled and slipped his arms around her waist. "In other words, the best of Sweetgrass." His gaze went distant. "Hmmm…"

"What are you thinking?"

He drew his attention back. "Well, if half the known universe will be there already, and we can pitch in to provide food, maybe Penny and I should give your idea serious consideration and bring in some key staffers who don't have other plans."

"But where will you house them?"

"Lodging, temporary and permanent, is high on my list of priorities for the town. Some bed and breakfasts, at a minimum."

"In all your spare time."

He caught the sarcasm and grinned. "Bridger and I talked earlier about some sort of temporary dormitory-type housing on the square—but I'd have to hire crews to construct them. There's no way we can get it done in time. Besides, Bridger's hell-bent to get a foundation poured on their house before Christmas. Assuming Penny will stop dinking with the house plans, that is." He paused. "I volunteered Ben and me to help him build it. Good practice for when we build our own."

She glanced around at the home where she'd raised her babies. It would be difficult to leave, but she understood Jackson's wish to make a home that was all their own. This had been the Butler homestead and David was a benevolent ghost, but his presence was never completely forgotten. Keeping him alive for his girls—and Ben, too—was important. David had been a good and decent man who'd stepped in when she was terrified and hopeless and had done right by her in so many ways.

It wasn't his fault he wasn't Jackson.

"We don't have to rush," Jackson reassured her. "We won't do it until you're ready."

"I'll be ready soon. I just—"

"You've had a lot thrown at you, too. Which reminds me, I am still determined to hire you some help around here. Not that I mind helping out, but—"

"Being a mogul is pretty time-consuming. Your company needs your attention."

"Not at your expense." He hesitated. "Vee, there's one thing I really want, though. It's the only thing I—" He didn't finish.

It was so out of character for Jackson to be tentative—about anything. "What is it?"

He kept one arm around her waist, and with the other hand, he lifted her left hand to his lips. "I want to put a ring on this finger. I want to know you're mine."

"Of course I'm yours." In a way she'd never fully forgive herself for, she always had been. She'd loved

David, but theirs had been a gentle, comfortable love that had grown over time. Jackson was the love of her life and had been since she was fifteen years old.

"I want this, Vee." He drew in a deep breath. "I…need it."

For such a strong, powerful man to make that admission was a sign of how seriously he took this. "I want to marry you, too. I just think it's important to give the kids time."

"I agree, but I'm Prince Daddy now, and Ben seems at peace—or as much so as a teenage boy can be. What are we waiting for?"

"I—"

"Be my Christmas present, Vee. Marry me for Christmas, would you? It's the only gift I want."

"How is it a gift, when you're the one with the magic wand and all the money?"

"I'm getting so much more." At her scoffing noise, he pressed the issue. "Sure, I have a lot of money and I can make life easier, but all you're reaping besides that is me. I'm gaining a whole family. Most of all, I'm getting you." His electric blue eyes were a magnet. Her lodestar. "I've needed you since the day I left, and I can never make it up to you that I did go, but—"

She hushed him with a finger to his lips. "We're past that now. I understand why you had to leave, and you couldn't know about Ben because I didn't." Even if she could have told him and brought him back, she hadn't known where to find him.

The pain of missing years of Ben's life turned his eyes dark. He closed them on an anguished exhale. "I can never, ever tell you how sorry I am."

She rose to her toes and kissed him softly. "We don't go back, Jackson. We have so much to look forward to."

"Does that mean you'll give me my perfect Christmas gift?"

"I'm hardly perfect." She winked. "It does save a lot of shopping, though. I mean, seriously—what do you give a gazillionaire?"

"You. You give him the love of his life. You walk down that aisle, and you let him pledge his life and his honor and his every last breath to you."

Her eyes overflowed. "I love you so much."

"Is that a yes?"

Through her tears, she found a chuckle. "That's a yes." Then her eyes flew open. "Dear heaven, do you know how little time we have to plan it? You don't mean actual Christmas, do you?"

"Why not? Everyone will already be here for this community Christmas. What better time?" He sobered. "Unless you want a fancy wedding. Vee, if you do, I'll give you the most elaborate wedding any woman ever imagined. Paris, Rome, London, Tahiti—you name it."

She covered her face with her hands. "I can't breathe."

"Why? What's wrong? Sweetheart, whatever you want, just name it. I'm sorry. I didn't mean to make you cry."

She uncovered her face to reveal helpless, half-hysterical laughter. "I don't want anywhere but Sweetgrass. But Jackson, how on earth will we manage—"

"Leave that to me." He shot her a cocky grin. "I have people."

"I need to sit down."

"I need to pick you up." Which he did, then began twirling her around the kitchen.

The kids came rushing. "What's going on?" Ben asked.

"Mommy, are you crying or laughing? What happened?"

"Your mommy just made me the happiest man in the world, punkin. She's going to marry me for Christmas."

"You can be like Scarlett, Mommy, in a beautiful princess gown!" Abby's eyes widened. "Beebee and me, we can be your flower girls! Want a beautiful dress, Beebee?"

Eyes equally wide, Beth nodded. "So you'll be our daddy for real, Prince Daddy?"

Jackson's gaze met Veronica's. "I want to adopt them. Will you let me?"

He would give them his heart either way, she knew. *Oh, David...* She wondered a little, but deep inside, she knew. David had grieved Jackson's leaving, too. They'd been friends since babyhood. "Of course."

"Yay!" Abby started skipping. "Ben! We get to be Gallaghers!"

Ben's eyes darkened, and he stiffened. "We're Butlers, Abby."

"Ben!"

"We're supposed to just forget Dad?" he shot back. Then he glanced at Jackson, his jaw mutinous. "He was Dad first."

"He was," Jackson acknowledged carefully and set her on her feet.

"You call Prince Daddy Dad," Abby reminded her brother. "He's your daddy now."

If anything, Ben's entire frame went more rigid.

Veronica ached for Jackson and Ben both. Ben had loved David with every fiber. He didn't know his birth father half so well. They were doing fine together most of the time, but the footing was still rocky. "Ben—"

Jackson stilled her with a hand on her arm. "Maybe we should talk about this later?" he asked Ben.

Ben only nodded once, briskly, then turned and ran upstairs to his room.

"I'm sorry." She saw Jackson's jaw flex and grieved for how this must hurt. Bad enough another man had raised his child, but to have that child reject the opportunity to be claimed legally? "It's—he's—"

Jackson shook his head, but his expression broke her heart.

"I'll go talk to him."

"No. Give him some space. I'm not forcing this on him. I have to earn it."

She touched his arm in sympathy. The muscles were stone-hard with tension.

Maybe he needed space, too. "Girls, it's time for your baths."

"Is Ben okay?" Abby queried.

"He's fine." Veronica took her by the hand to lead her upstairs. She turned to reach for Beth, only to see her daughter standing by Jackson silently, holding onto his leg as if offering support. Jackson was staring down at the top of her blonde head, his big hand cradled protectively over her hair.

"We'll be upstairs, Beth," she said softly. With her eyes, she gave Jackson a kiss of comfort.

Chapter Two

As the last few customers trickled out, the cleanup began. Ian was waiting to take Scarlett home, bantering with Jeanette and Henry and Brenda while helping them out, turning chairs on top of tables so the dishwasher Pete could mop.

Weary and a little lightheaded, Scarlett pushed to get done sooner. Her feet hurt, her back ached and she was more than ready for bed. While sharpening her favorite knife, she lost her grip and grabbed for it. Pain struck, and she gasped. A thin red line of blood appeared on her palm. Her right palm. Her dominant hand. If she'd lost the use of it, even for a day, with all she had to accomplish—

For a second she couldn't breathe. She closed her eyes and focused on settling down her heart. *One…breath…one…*

"What the hell—" Instantly Ian was beside her, one arm sliding around her waist as he grabbed for her hand and turned the palm upward. He swore while reaching for a paper towel. "Brenda, the first aid kit—now!" he snapped.

He turned her in his arms. "You need to sit down.

33

Hell, you need to forget about this place," he growled.

Between her fears and his fury, she couldn't settle the heart that was already pounding in double time.

"Ian, I—" Helplessly she batted at his hands. Sucked in air she couldn't find. Wrenched herself from his arms when what she desperately wanted was to curl up there for week, months…forever. "I'm fine. I'm fine." She held up a hand to forestall all the concern being directed her way.

"You are not fine. Give me your hand." When she didn't immediately comply, his own was lightning-quick to seize hers. As he bent to clean the blood and bandage the wound, his voice was sharp. "You're working too damn hard, and our baby—"

She covered her eyes with her free hand as hot tears formed. He was voicing her own terror. She desperately wanted this baby, but she'd promised Nana she would save Sweetgrass with this events center and she would, come hell or high water.

"Henry—" Ian barked. "You all finish it. I'm taking Scarlett home."

She whirled on him. "Don't! You're part of the problem, don't you see, Ian? You want me tucked away home, sitting in a rocking chair and—and—" She threw out her uninjured hand. "Knitting or—" Anger made her heedless. "I am not some delicate flower! Maddie has three children with one on the way, and she runs her cafe just fine! I am not helpless!"

The entire room had gone still. She and Ian disagreed at times, but never like this. Never…shouting. She could feel all their eyes on her.

That only made her more furious. "Don't stop! We have too much to do—we—"

It was Jeanette who hazarded to approach her. "Scarlett, it's okay," she said calmly but without pity in her voice. Scarlett couldn't tolerate pity. "You're under a lot of pressure, but you're not looking at the difference in your situations. Maddie is not trying to run two restaurants, especially not one with the unbearable burden of being the salvation of Sweetgrass. You're carrying a much heavier load, and you need to face facts: it's not necessary. Jackson's bringing in business and jobs, and others will follow. It's not all on you anymore."

She looked Scarlett straight in the eye. "I know you and I don't get along most of the time, but maybe that very thing will convince you I'm not saying this to be nice. You want the honest truth? It never was all on you. Sweetgrass has survived for a long time before you ever showed up."

The rebuke stung. "But—" Scarlett glanced away. "I promised Nana. This is her dream."

"You know that's not true," Jeanette snapped. "At least half of this is your ambition speaking. You've got your Paris-trained-chef superhero cape on when you think like that. You know good and well what Ruby wants most from you is to be here, to be healthy and happy...to *stay*, Scarlett. That's it, the whole shebang: for you to stay. Not for you to singlehandedly carry Sweetgrass on your shoulders."

Hurt and angry, Scarlett glared at Ian. "Did you put her up to this?"

He reared back as if she'd slapped him. "I don't ask

other people to fight my battles for me. You know that."

She did know. Ian was the original knight in shining armor, the one who battled everyone else's dragons. She knew—*knew*—how hard he'd been biting his tongue as day after day she battled morning sickness and fatigue, struggling to find some balance between all her commitments and the part of her that wanted to simply curl up in his arms and never leave. To focus on growing the baby she so deeply cherished.

But she'd promised Nana…and Nana needed her.

Then Brenda, little quiet as a mouse Brenda, of all people, spoke up. "Maybe the cafe could close at night. If breakfast and lunch were served here and dinner over there, we could all work both places instead of being split up."

Scarlett had had the same thought. "But everyone in town counts on the cafe to be open for supper. Ruby's Dream is going to be too high-end for their budgets."

"Does it have to be?" Brenda asked.

Scarlett stared at the meek girl whose past was such a mystery.

She frowned. "We need people coming from Austin and San Antonio to make it work. To provide the market for the ranchers' beef and the farmers' organic produce."

"But isn't—" Brenda seemed to be summoning every last ounce of courage to argue. "Isn't there a compromise? Can't you let it grow from something small to something bigger and fancier later, if that's what you want?"

"And who says Ruby's Dream has to be open right away, anyhow?" Jeanette demanded. Her eyes narrowed.

"You know who's all bent out of shape over that. It's not Ruby."

"But—" She'd been so focused. She'd wanted it open in October. "I promised Jackson it would be here when he started bringing in employees, so they could see this wasn't a cultural and gastronomic wasteland. Plus I told him I'd cater his company Christmas party."

"Jackson can deal," Ian said impatiently. "Hell, he's got the money to fly in food, for that matter."

"But that's not the point—"

"What is the point?" he demanded. "How much farther do you have to push yourself to prove whatever the hell it is you're trying to prove?"

"Ian, you don't understand—"

"I understand plenty, first of which is I'm taking you home. Right this minute." Without waiting for her to respond, he scooped her up and stalked out the door.

She sat across the truck from him, a study in stiff, silent misery. Those delicate shoulders that tried to hold up the world were hunched as if to protect herself from a blow. One pale, slim hand curved over the small bump that was their baby's living cradle, and Ian couldn't stand how much she was hurting.

Or the fact that he was the cause of much of it.

Time after time, words rushed to the tip of his tongue. *I'm not the enemy. You have to take better care of yourself. They don't deserve you.*

Hell, *he* didn't deserve her. But he had her, and he wasn't letting go, by God.

At last he pulled up to the ranch house and parked. She remained staring ahead, no telling what was charging through that busy brain of hers. The woman barely slept, as it was. He couldn't be robbing her of more rest by making her upset. But—

"Damn it—" He slammed a fist on the wheel. "This has to end."

And immediately felt like crap as she lifted that small, courageous chin in defiance.

Protecting herself. Distancing herself.

From him.

"I'm sorry." With a gust of resignation, he got out and walked around before she could step down. When he reached for her, she stiffened, and something inside him died. "I'm not the enemy, sweetheart," he said gruffly as his voice tightened against the misery. "Please. Let me take you inside." He waited, clearly ready to scoop her up but trying like hell to restrain himself, to let her choose, though everything inside him ached and growled and readied itself to battle all comers for her.

I don't need a white knight, Ian. How many times had she said that to him?

But you do, my love. Because you won't protect yourself. You lay yourself on the line every damn day…

He lost his patience and swept her up in his arms. Carried her inside and up the stairs with only a nod at his dad, who sat in the living room, reading.

Gordon's brows lifted, concern on his features. As if asking if she was hurt.

With a quick shake of his head, determined not to stop their progress, Ian kept going. He would explain later. Right now, Scarlett was all he could see. All he could feel.

She perched in his arms, still stiff with resentment. He knew their battle wasn't over—and damned himself for adding to her misery when all he wanted to do was help.

Inside their room, door pushed shut with one boot, Scarlett squirmed to get down, and he almost let her.

But distance was not what they needed. No walls thrown up to barricade them from the essential truth.

They loved each other.

But she was killing herself trying to prove her love to everyone. All the time.

So Ian kept a tight grip on her. "Hush now," he said in the most soothing voice he could muster. He had to focus on being calm himself if he hoped to ever get her to settle down. She was stubborn as ten mules, and most times, that determination served her well. Made her capable of accomplishing more than whole groups of people combined.

But right now, she needed to listen—to herself. To her body.

And, please God, to him. Because he couldn't take watching her do this to herself anymore.

He sat down in the big rocker they'd moved into the room, anticipating their baby's arrival. It was big and stuffed and wrapped around you like loving arms. Scarlett had taken to sitting there with a cup of tea some nights as they traded news of the day or talked about the future, about whether they wanted to know if they were having a girl or a boy. She was scared to try to raise a boy but wanted one for him. He didn't care, as long as she and the child were healthy and safe. The image of a little girl with Scarlett's ebony curls and clear blue eyes had the power to stop him in his tracks, to make his heart ache with the urge to cuddle and defend.

He heaved a sigh. But the baby's health was only part of what they were here to settle. "I'm worried about you," he admitted.

"You always are." She was still stiff with misery and anger.

He drew her close, decided to be smarter than he usually was, and shut the hell up. Instead, he used one boot—damn it, he'd forgotten to take it off and there was mud clinging to the side, but no way was he taking it off now. He knew how to mop.

He set them rocking, and he began to stroke her, head to foot.

Every trailing glide down her back made him settle a little more, and she, too, began to relax. They rocked in silence for several minutes, and every time words rose to his throat, he ruthlessly quashed them. Touch was doing what words would not, calming her down. Calming him down. He snuggled her closer into his chest.

At last she rested her head on his shoulder and gave up the fight. When she drifted off to sleep, he knew he'd sit in this chair all night long, if that's what it took to give her the peace and sleep she so desperately needed. With one hand, he covered their baby in her belly and rocked them both slowly.

Then he felt a faint flutter. For the very first time.

Ian swore his heart stopped. He kept his hand there, going as still as he could manage, listening hard, though he understood logically that listening wasn't going to help.

Again, little one. Please. Let me feel you once more.

A second tiny ripple, as delicate as a butterfly's wings.

Hello, little one.

His heart… Had there ever been a feeling like this?

"Did you just feel…?" Scarlett's husky voice asked.

His eyes locked on hers. "Have you ever—?"

She shook her head. "Not—I didn't realize…" Tears sprang to her eyes, and he felt his own burn.

Then there she was, pressing into his chest, arms flung around his neck. Trembling.

"I love you," she said softly. "I'm sorry. I just—"

"Shh…" He gathered her more tightly into himself, as though somehow it were possible to dissolve the barriers of flesh and become fully one. He closed his eyes and spoke from the heart. "I don't want to clip your wings. I want you to fly as high as you want. I know you've given up every dream you ever had to stay here with me, and I'll spend my life making it up to you—"

She reared back, eyes wet, and pressed one palm to his cheek. "You're my dream. You and—wow." She glanced down. "I…I don't…"

He smiled at her. "I know. She's real. We're going to have a baby, Scarlett." His voice thickened. "I never knew I could love like this. I didn't know happiness like you existed. If I'm overbearing and too protective, it's

41

only because—"

She kissed him, and it was sweet and it made him ache.

He yanked her to him, buried his head in her shoulder. "I can't lose you, Scarlett. I have to keep you safe if you won't do it for yourself, but I don't want to make you stop loving me. I only—"

One small hand tightened on the back of his neck, and she sighed from deep inside. "Jeanette's right. Ambition was my driving force for so long because it was the only way I knew to hide how lonely I was after Mama was gone. It was just me, and I thought I'd be alone forever. So I worked. I became really, really good at one thing. And then when I found Nana, I knew I'd do whatever it took not to disappoint her or she might…" He heard her swallow hard. "It's embarrassing to be a grown woman and feel this, but a part of me keeps waiting to be sent away. To have to remember how to be alone again. So I work, to make sure I'm never helpless."

He sat up and brought her face up to his. "You will never have to be alone or feel helpless again. Ruby will die one day—" He heard her exclamation of dismay. "You know she won't live forever. Do you honestly think that what she wants as her legacy is a restaurant? You're her legacy, Scarlett, and our baby extends her footprint into time. Because you're here, Ruby's line doesn't end with her passing. You've given her a future and hope. Now give her some of your time, and not in front of a stove. Let her be your grandmother, let her fuss over you—hell, let *me* fuss over you. Best I can tell, you were the adult in your little family as often as your mom was. Have you ever let anyone else take care of you, really? Do you not get that I'm hardwired to do that? That I consider it my finest duty and my most important job? Especially now, when you're carrying a part of me inside you, could you please let us both enjoy this special time instead of working yourself into the ground?"

She sighed and sagged against him. "I don't know how I can."

He started them rocking again. "I can talk to Jackson and explain. He'll understand. And I'll talk to Ruby when she gets home in a couple of days."

"No."

He frowned. Glanced down.

She started smiling. Used her thumb to rub away the line between his brows. "You are so fierce. Why did I ever think you were easygoing?"

"Because compared to you, I'm a Zen master?" But he grinned. "Okay, why no?"

She started to sit up, then fell back against him. "This feels good. I don't want to move."

He smiled. "Please don't. I like it, too." He kept rocking. Waited.

At last she spoke. "I know you want to protect me, but I can't become a kept woman."

Laughter burst from his throat.

"What?"

"A kept woman. I wish." Deep laughter rolled through him again. "Sweetheart, you would have to have a brain transplant to be passive. No offense."

"I love your dimple." She traced it with one finger. "Have I mentioned that lately?"

That dimple had once embarrassed the living daylights out of him, but he was all about the dimple now, if that kept her attention on him. "Once or twice." Then he couldn't stand it—he had to kiss her. The kiss turned long and lascivious. He gathered her closer and delighted when she squirmed and tried to get closer still.

"Wait—" She pushed at his chest. "I have to say this one thing."

"Now?"

She laughed at what he knew was a pained expression. He wanted her naked. This. Second.

"Don't be a baby. Man up."

He sighed and laid his head back on the rocker. "Spill."

"You're right that I have to find a new path. I can't bear to think of not opening Ruby's Dream until after the baby is born, and I'm not admitting defeat yet, but— I'll consider it." She play-smacked his chest. "Don't grin. It's not becoming."

"Not grinning. Wouldn't dream of it." But inside he was tap-dancing.

"You are not talking to Jackson or Nana on my behalf. I'm a big girl and a professional. Yes, they're family, but this is business, too."

"But you will talk to them? Cut yourself some slack? 'Cause I'm not going to wait forever. If you don't, I will."

"Down, Cro-Magnon. Yes, I'll talk to them."

"When?"

She began unbuttoning her blouse. "Not before I have my way with you. You okay with that?"

"Thank heaven." He sent a glance of fervent gratitude skyward. "I am all over that." He tried to help her unbutton to hurry things up, and their fingers tangled. He swore and rose, still holding her.

Then tossed her on the bed. "Oh, no—" He froze. "Can we do this? Did I hurt you?"

She stripped off her yoga pants while she smiled. "If Mama ain't happy, ain't nobody happy, isn't that the saying?" She crooked a finger. "Get naked and get over here. Don't make me come after you."

He was naked and had her naked seconds later. "You're so scary," he said, as he nipped at her thigh.

Scarlett giggled and grinned...until she moaned.

Chapter Three

"What are you doing here? And where's Scarlett?"

Standing at the grill in the diner the next morning, Penny jolted. "Aunt Ruby! Where did you come from? You're not due in until tomorrow. What bride does that, comes home early from her honeymoon?"

"I don't suppose you'd know, seein's how you won't set a date with that poor Bridger. What are you waiting on, missy? Think a better man is gonna drop in your lap?"

"No." Penny tried to keep the surly teenager out of her voice, but Aunt Ruby was making her feel cornered. "We'll get to it. And no, there's no better man, and you know it." She sniffed. "The holidays aren't a good time for a wedding."

Aunt Ruby snorted. "Any time is a good one when you've got a man like that waiting."

"Says the woman who kept Arnie on a string for eighteen years."

"Don't be impertinent."

They grinned at each other, delighted with the impasse. There was nothing quite like a good, rousing challenge, Penny thought.

Ruby frowned. "I repeat: why are you here? Is something wrong with my granddaughter?"

Ian had called this morning while Scarlett slept in and explained the situation, asking if she'd help out.

"Scarlett's fine, but we voted her a day off." She crossed one set of fingers behind her back for the lie. "What do you think I'm doing? I'm cooking. I happen to be good at it—maybe not Scarlett-good or Ruby-good, but better than Rissa." She snickered.

Aunt Ruby joined her laughter. "Poor child. You'd think a stove was a pit of vipers."

Penny sobered. "She really didn't have a chance to learn. She was only twelve when Mama died and—" Both women sighed. The story of the fragmentation of the Gallagher family was an old and sad one.

"Well," Ruby said, patting her shoulder. "You're all back together now. Mary would be so pleased."

"I miss my mother so much," Penny admitted. "Even after all this time."

"That never goes away, honey." Ruby was no doubt thinking of her own lost daughter Georgia, Scarlett's mother. "You just have to remember the love. No one loved better than your mama."

Suddenly, Penny remembered a Christmas custom from her childhood. "Could we have a Cookie Day?"

"Your mama did that every year. The whole bunch of you, and she always invited in a few strays like me."

"You couldn't be a stray if you tried, Aunt Ruby." Penny hugged the tiny woman.

"Cookie Day?" Brenda appeared in the doorway.

"What's that?" Then she spotted Ruby and beamed. "Ruby! You're home!" She started to approach, then hesitated.

"Oh, get yourself over here, girl. I missed you." Ruby opened her arms wide and gathered in the girl. Penny wondered if Brenda was even out of her teens yet, but nobody knew.

Then Brenda drew back. "Have you heard about the Christmas dinner yet? Oh, Ruby, it's going to be great!" Normally so quiet and shy, her pale, near-white hair and slender frame making her seem even more fragile, this Brenda was lit by an inner flame.

"What Christmas dinner?"

"Not for you to fix," Penny hastened to explain. "A community Christmas meal, and everybody's contributing."

Brenda drew a notepad from her apron. "I'm making a list—see?" Her forehead furrowed. "I think we're going to have too much potato salad." She grimaced, then brightened. "But plenty of jello salad! I like jello salad. Once I knew this lady who fixed them every Sunday."

"Someone in your family?" Ruby asked. Like Penny and everyone else, curiosity reigned concerning this quiet girl who'd shown up one day, bruised and jumpy. Ruby, the saint of strays, had taken her in and given her a job and, more importantly, a place to belong.

But still, no one knew anything about her past or where she came from.

"Just…" Brenda shrugged. "One of the moms."

"In foster care?" Penny ventured.

Brenda ducked her head, every trace of joy dimming.

"Doesn't matter. So tell me who's bringing dessert so far," Ruby prodded.

Brenda perked up. "Well, Melba Sykes is bringing this orange date cake she says is a family tradition."

"Oh, that's a good one. You'll like that, I bet."

Brenda nodded. "And Granny Cosgrove is going to make a bread pudding, and Raymond Benefield says he'll contribute a fruitcake."

Ruby snorted. "He most certainly will not. He's been trying to pawn off that fruitcake every year since God was a pup."

Brenda's eyes rounded. "But...how can I tell him no?"

"You won't have to. I'll take care of it when he shows up for breakfast tomorrow. I will not have him poisoning anybody on Christmas."

"Oh, and there's going to be a tree in the courthouse, and one outside, too." Brenda was practically vibrating with excitement.

"Are we having a tree trimming? Might be a nice way to end Cookie Day. We can bake over here and at the courthouse kitchen. Mary would like that, don't you think?"

"She sure would," Penny answered.

"So what's Cookie Day?" Brenda asked.

"When I was growing up, my mother set aside a whole day for the entire family to bake cookies of all kinds. Each of us picked one recipe, and we worked together to make them. Then we would assemble plates with an assortment and we'd take them around to folks who didn't have family and to our friends."

"Oh! Could we do that? All of us?" Brenda's face fell. "But I'm not a Gallagher."

"We're all Gallaghers on Cookie Day, right, Penny?" Henry said fiercely, always ready to leap to Brenda's aid.

"Absolutely. Heaven help you." Penny smiled as Ruby chuckled. "But you two have to help me out so Scarlett doesn't wind up doing all the work. You know how she is about taking responsibility. Matter of fact, I think that's the first rule. Scarlett can pick a recipe to make, but only one. We can't have her working herself to the bone any worse than she already does. Ruby either. You two with me on this?"

"Yes, ma'am."

She looked askance at him. "Henry, what have I told you about calling me ma'am?"

The young man flushed. "Sorry, ma—Penny."

"That's better."

Then her phone sounded with her brother's ringtone, and she tapped her bluetooth. "Sand tarts still your favorite cookie, Jackson?"

"What?" her twin asked. "Where are you?"

"I'm cooking at the diner. And planning Cookie Day. What are you doing?"

"Well, I was trying to plan a new promotional campaign for the *Doom Galaxy* launch—" He began laughing. "We've kinda fallen down the rabbit hole, haven't we, sis?"

She understood exactly. "High finance, world domination…and Cookie Day. Just another day in Sweetgrass, bro."

She grinned at the sound of his laughter, the twin she'd lost for half their lives, the man who'd come to Sweetgrass shrouded in mystery and so long estranged from everyone and everything familiar.

"All we need to complete the chaos is to put Abby in charge."

"Hey, I have plans for that girl," she responded. "She reminds me of me."

"Stop. You'll give me nightmares," Jackson responded. Abby was a force of nature, for sure. Her brother would have his hands full, raising her. "Cookie Day, huh? When?"

She glanced over at Brenda and Henry. "What do you think? Just under three weeks left before Christmas. This weekend?"

"Yes!" Brenda clapped her hands, looking more like a girl than ever.

Ruby was shaking her head and muttering, no doubt thinking about the logistics.

But Penny was all about the organizing. She'd make this work.

"Why do I think this won't be happening in the kitchen at the ranch?" Jackson asked.

"And you the big mogul world traveler. Gotta think big, brother mine. Downtown Sweetgrass, at Ruby's and Ruby's Dream."

"Two commercial kitchens?" Jackson whistled. "So the whole town is coming?"

"Wouldn't surprise me in the least," she said.

"Me either."

"So why did you call?"

"Well…" He cleared his throat. "I wanted to tell you first. Vee's agreed to marry me."

"Where's the surprise in that? Not that I'm not happy."

"That's the thing. I want to do it at Christmas. While everyone's in town already."

"Christmas?" Not a lot flabbergasted her, but—"*This* Christmas? Would Veronica like some help clubbing you over the head?"

"She was having a little trouble breathing," he admitted. "But I can afford to pay for speed."

Ruby appeared to be about to explode with curiosity. Brenda was frozen in place.

Jeanette walked to the window. "Where's my order?"

"Brother mine, you are such a guy. How can anyone so smart be this clueless? I have to cook now, but you'd better get yourself down here *tout de suite*, hear me? On second thought, Veronica's the one who needs to be here. You just get ready to open that big, fat wallet of yours."

"Penny, it's going to be okay. I've got this."

"Don't be an idiot. You and Veronica be here in thirty minutes. The breakfast rush is almost over. Don't make me hurt you."

"Should I point out that I'm your employer?"

Her eyes went to slits. "Not for long. I have low tolerance for stupidity." She disconnected. Saw her rapt audience, but moved first to slide eggs on a plate and add toast. "Jeanette, how long did it take you to make Scarlett's dress?"

"What? Oh, don't tell me Bridger finally—"

"Not me. My bonehead twin. He's convinced Veronica to marry him at Christmas."

"*This* Christmas?" echoed every woman in the vicinity.

"Exactly. We have to rally round. The man's clearly got more money than brains." Evil glee filled her. "We're going to help out this poor woman who obviously does not understand that she's made a bad bargain. Are we agreed, ladies?"

"And here I thought that boy was smart," Ruby muttered. "We'd best get Maddie on the phone, too."

Jeanette turned away with her order. Brenda had stars in her eyes.

Penny wanted to put a knot on her brother's thick skull. Then she cackled and punched in the number for Rissa.

Word began to spread like wildfire.

Jackson and Veronica stopped stock-still when they entered Ruby's Diner.

The main room was full. Scarlett and Ian, Rissa and Mackey, Ruby and Arnie, Jeanette, Henry, Brenda, Bridger...plus everyone from the breakfast bunch who'd lingered, as though they would never be allowed coffee again if they left.

Along with everyone they could manage to call as the news spread.

"Do we have to make a big deal of this?" Jackson

winced as he escorted Veronica through the door.

"A better question: is anyone left to keep things running anywhere in this town or the surroundings?" Rissa smirked as she walked over to hug her older brother, then sock him on the shoulder.

"Ouch."

"Consider yourself lucky." She pointed to Veronica. "She should be doing worse to you."

Penny bent to Scarlett, standing beside her. "Serves him right," she muttered. Scarlett snickered.

"Right over here, Man of the Hour." Penny gestured him to a spot reserved for the prospective bride and groom.

"Seriously, did every ranch and business in town just close for the day?" Jackson asked, scanning the room.

"Pretty much," Mackey chimed in. "What? You thought you'd do this on your own? With this bunch of meddlers?"

"Guess not," Jackson sighed. "I thought maybe Vee and I could work with a wedding planner or something."

"You've been gone too long, boy," chimed in Harley Sykes. "You're in Sweetgrass now. You belong to us."

Beside Penny, Bridger grinned, his expression slightly dazzled. The man who'd wanted exactly this sort of community must be in hog heaven right now.

He'd been right when he'd once said there was nothing normal about Sweetgrass. Especially when the prodigal son and the town's sweetheart were about to marry.

"We thought we'd keep it simple," Veronica protested. "Just a little ceremony sometime around the community Christmas, so everyone could be here."

"And there's where your thinking went off the rails," Rissa said. "Sweetgrass? Simple? So not happening."

Ian spoke up from the other side of Scarlett. "I have one requirement. Scarlett and Ruby do not cater. They're guests." His jaw set. "Nonnegotiable."

Scarlett sighed. "I thought you were going to let me deal with this," she muttered.

Ian merely crossed his arms. "So I'm Cro-Magnon."

Scarlett grinned. But didn't argue, astonishingly.

Well, then.

"You could save everybody an extra trip and make it a double wedding, Penny," Shirley Carpenter offered.

Penny froze. Bridger darted a glance at her. She knew what he was thinking and waited for him to agree.

"Ms. Penelope and I will make our own plans, thank you," he responded easily, though she felt the tension in his frame. "I'm holding out for a beach wedding. With bikinis. On everyone."

They all laughed, and she managed a smile, but she knew he'd be so much happier if she'd pipe up and agree that Shirley's idea was a great one.

Jackson studied her, concern in his eyes, but she had some questions for her twin herself. Something was off with him and Veronica, she could sense it in the old twin way that had once made them privy to one another's every thought, but she couldn't figure the source of the uneasiness.

She tuned back in as Jeanette volunteered to fashion Veronica a gown.

Jackson shook his head. "I know I've messed up everything by pushing to do it by Christmas. You can't possibly have time, Jeanette, as busy as you are. I'll fly Veronica to New York or Paris or have samples flown in here for her."

"I don't want anything fancy," Veronica protested.

It was easy to see that Jackson wanted to give her the world, however. "Abby is set on you having a princess gown like Scarlett, remember?"

"I can do it," Jeanette offered. "Come to my house later today, and we can at least talk about it. I can't produce a billionaire bridal gown, but—"

"Scarlett's was absolutely gorgeous," Veronica said. "I know you'd do a beautiful one, but it's not fair to you."

"You let me be the judge of that."

Penny spoke up. "Jackson, you could bring in seamstresses to help once Jeanette's designed it. That might help her out."

"I won't need—"

"Jeanette," Scarlett said gently. "Let Jackson pay his penance if you wind up needing the help."

"There are several good seamstresses in town," Melba remarked. "We can help her just fine." She turned to Jeanette. "What we can't do is design like you can. You have no business waiting tables."

But what on earth would they do if she left the diner? Penny thought.

"They won't let me cook," Rissa piped up. "But I can smack Harley in line nearly as well as you can. I can take some of your hours."

Well. That was unexpected.

Scarlett spoke then. "One cranky waitress for another. No one will ever notice."

The room filled with chuckles.

As the laughter slowed, Penny heard Jackson again. "No expense spared, Jeanette. Sky's the limit on fabrics. Anything you need, you ask, and I'll make it happen."

The glow on Jeanette's face didn't slip past Ruby or Scarlett, Penny could see.

"I knew we'd lose her sooner or later," Scarlett said. "Who could have imagined I'd be sad?"

"Girl's needed to leave Sweetgrass for years," Ruby added. "Hayley's been after her to come to L.A."

"Hayley." Scarlett's face darkened.

Penny snickered.

"Wait 'til she's flirting with your man, missy," Scarlett warned.

"But she's got fabulous shoes," Penny said. "Give the woman her due."

Bridger chuckled beside her.

The planning went on. Brenda asked shyly if Veronica would let her help with the flowers. Jackson insisted that Veronica not be working on her wedding day and promised to get together with Brenda later.

"Hey! I can bake the cake," Rissa volunteered.

With Eric's lopsided, runny-icing birthday cake fresh in everyone's minds, laughter erupted again.

"You're all heart, babe," Mackey said, tugging at her ponytail.

"I was serious," Rissa grumbled.

Then laughed straight from the belly.

Chapter Four

Afterward, when Veronica left to get back to her greenhouses, Jackson headed for the kitchen at Scarlett's request. He winked as he passed Penny.

Love looked good on her twin. It softened the tense, ragged edges Jackson had arrived in town with.

She smiled at her brother and blew him a kiss.

He nodded and smiled back, but she could see a strain she didn't understand, and she worried. She'd talk to him about it, first chance. Maybe there was something she could do to help. He was carrying a lot on those broad shoulders.

"Penny for your thoughts," said Bridger from behind her, sliding his arms around her waist. "Pun intended."

She turned to him, newly aware of how easily this could be lost. "I love you. And you know I want us to be together, right? But I don't want a double wedding. Is that awful?"

"You should be the star of your own show, Legs. It's okay, really."

She could see it in his eyes, though, the longing to make their relationship official. To settle down. He'd never had that.

"Stop worrying," he said. "I'm okay. I don't care what Shirley thinks. I'm not in love with Shirley."

"It would be easier, though. Shirley's simple."

Bridger hooted. "Shirley is a busybody with a Machiavellian mind for gossip and intrigue." He kissed her forehead. "Ditch the frown. I like my bluetooth-addicted, stiletto-wearing cook just fine." He glanced down. "I thought you seemed shorter. What happened?"

"My feet hurt."

"So you're cooking in red cowboy boots? Most folks who have to be on their feet all day at work wear something with more support."

"I cook with style, country boy."

"You do everything with style, Shark Girl. Want to go off in the corner and neck?" He pressed his mouth to her throat and had her moaning.

"Good goshomighty, have you two no shame?" Rissa hollered.

"Get your own hottie," Penny shouted right back.

"Funny about that," her sister retorted. "Mackey, where are you?"

"Penny, may I have a word with you?" Joyce Walden asked, Linda Vise beside her.

Uh-oh. "I'm helping at the cafe. I can't come to quilting."

Joyce smiled. "We're not going to kidnap you. We only want your help with something. We'd like to make a quilt for Veronica and Jackson."

"I thought you weren't going to kidnap me."

"I suspect you'll want to help when you hear what we're planning." Earlene Dorsa, Ruth Sudduth, Linda

Johnson, Ceci Sinnwell and Melba Sykes joined them.

"What?"

"We each have pieces in our fabric stashes that were used in quilts we did with your mother, but we'd like something of hers to put in it. It would be a double wedding ring quilt."

"Do you have time to do that before the wedding?"

"It's going to be tight. Mary wouldn't mind us piecing it on the machine—we couldn't possibly finish in time, otherwise—but we must quilt it by hand, as she would want."

"So what do you need from me?"

"We would like you to quilt at least a little section in honor of your mother. She would have wanted this."

She would have. "All right."

"But first we need you to find us fabric from something of hers."

Penny went still. When her mother died, they'd all been so grief-stricken. She barely remembered some of her mother's friends coming over to help pack things up. Rissa had been inconsolable. Had unpacked some of the boxes as quickly as they'd filled until Dad had made her let the women work. Remembering that period was painful still. "I have no idea if anything was even kept."

"We boxed up her fabric stash for you girls," Jane Shurtleff said. "I'm sure it's there somewhere."

"Really?" What else of her mother's might still be at the ranch?

And why hadn't she thought to ask until now?

Jackson's battles with their father had escalated after their mother's death. Then the accident. Penny had been trying to help out, to cook, to be their mother's substitute while keeping up her schoolwork—

Then Jackson had vanished.

She'd consoled a terrified, heartbroken Clary.

But she'd left for freshman orientation the week after graduation. She'd hardly ever returned home.

"Will you look, please? And could you do it right away, you and Rissa? This would mean a lot to your mother."

It would. Of that, Penny had no doubt. *Oh, Mama.*

"I'll go to the ranch right now," she promised.

At the Star Bar G, she found her father first. "Daddy, what happened to Mother's things?"

Nothing was more guaranteed to make the man freeze up. "Why do you want to know?"

She explained about the quilt, regretting that it clearly caused him pain, even after all these years.

"There are boxes in the attic," he said gruffly. "I've never opened them. I...couldn't." He cleared his throat and glanced away.

She thought about losing Bridger, as unformed and newborn as their love was, and she comprehended in a whole new way the blow her mother's loss would have been to her dad. She barely knew Bridger in comparison, but she would never get over losing him, the light he cast, the safety he granted, the humor and warmth he'd brought into her life.

Her mother had been their beacon. Their shining light.

"I'm sorry," she said to her father. "I didn't understand until now what you must have gone through."

Her father's gaze whipped to hers, surprisingly vulnerable. "Your mama was everything." He cleared his throat again. "Damn sure too good for me."

"She loved you so much." She saw his head turn toward her like a flower to sunlight. As if he needed to hear this.

"I wasn't good enough to her. Or for her."

"She thought you were."

"You were a child."

But Penny knew she was right. "Remember how she'd tease you and say *oh, you*, then flutter her hand like this?" Penny demonstrated something she'd seen a thousand times in her life, her mother's gentle remonstration, her flirting reprimand when he tried to scandalize her. There had been humor between them. No one else could make her father laugh, really, not the way Mama had.

His smile was soft and sad. "She tried to make a better man of me." He heaved a sigh. "She wouldn't be proud of how I handled her children." He shook his bowed head.

"We've all fallen in love now. Maybe we can't know exactly how it was with the two of you, but when I think of how I would feel if Bridger—" The very notion sent a shaft of terror through her.

"You never get over it," her father said quietly. "The hole your mama left...but I still should have done better." His head rose, his gaze sharpening. "So what's the holdup with you?"

"What do you mean?"

"Don't try to fake me out, Princess. You were never any good at it. A blind man could see how eager Bridger is to marry you. He's a good guy. What's your problem?"

Penny shook her head slowly. "I don't—" She met her father's eyes, wishing her mother were here. She'd know what to do. "I love him Daddy, I really do." She shrugged. "Anyway, it's Jackson's turn now. I am not going to compete with that. He and Veronica have lost too much time together. He wants this to be special, and I'm not horning in on it."

"Want your own spotlight, Princess?"

"No!" She shrugged and smiled. "I don't know. Maybe. I'm not sure what's the right thing to do. This is so important to Bridger, but I'll never be his Suzy Homemaker."

"Pretty sure he's not asking you to."

"You're right. It's just—" She exhaled. "There's an awful lot of emotion swirling around right now, Daddy. I quit letting myself get all emotional a long time ago."

Her father snorted. "You are not pulling the wool over my eyes. You've always felt a lot behind that ice princess mask you wore. You just don't like making yourself vulnerable. You count on being in control."

"You know me too well. I'm working on it, but…I wish I were more like Mama."

"You are, Princess. You only thought you didn't want to be. I didn't give your mama much of a life here, working so hard to help me make this place profitable, raising you kids, keeping all of us happy… She deserved better."

"She always said she was right where she wanted to be."

His gaze was surprisingly open. "You think that's true?" He seemed to really want to know.

"I do. Sure, her life required a lot of hard work, but Mama was all about love, and she had a whole batch of us to love, didn't she?"

"Spread it to everyone she possibly could," he agreed.

Just then the school bus lumbered to a stop, and Eric raced off. "Grandpa! Guess what happened today?"

Her father turned with a smile. "I'm betting you're gonna tell me, aren't you?"

"I sure am." Eric started running toward them. "Hi, Aunt Penny!"

The boy had blossomed, and they'd all marveled at the relationship between her father and Rissa's adopted son. "Hey, yourself. Have a good day at school?"

"Yeah!" Then he deflated. "'Cept for stupid English. Who cares about verbs and nouns? I know how to speak English just fine."

She slapped a hand over her heart. "Words are my life. You're stabbing me straight in the heart, young man. Anyway, how am I going to make you into a world-class shark lawyer if you don't learn grammar?"

"I'm gonna be a SEAL, remember? Like my dad." Every time Eric said the words *dad* or *mom* or *grandpa*, it was as though he'd uttered something holy.

"I thought you were going to train horses like your

mom."

"After I'm a SEAL," he said patiently, as though she were a little thick.

She chuckled. "I'm pretty sure even SEALs care about grammar. They learn other languages, too, you know."

His little nose wrinkled. "Oh, maaaan. *Two* sets of nouns and verbs and junk?"

Her father laughed and ruffled Eric's hair. "Maybe a cookie would help, you think? Celia made some just a little while ago."

The housekeeper Celia's daughter Samantha caught up then. "Eric, I made a ninety-eight on my grammar test."

"And you still can't be a SEAL," he taunted. "'Cause you're a stupid ole girl."

"I can so, any day now. Mackey told me. Mackey! Where are you?" She took off running in search of the man who had just poked his head out of the barn.

"Dad, tell her," Eric called out. "I can be a SEAL right now, but she can't, right?"

Mackey grinned, shaking his head. "Dude, what I have I told you about that?"

"Maybe I'd best go help out," her father said, clearly eager to be with Eric. "You need anything else, Princess?"

"No, thanks. I'll just go look in the attic."

"Your sister might want to help."

"I can see she's busy with a horse right now, but would you ask her to join me when she can?"

"Sure will." His step was lighter and more eager than

she'd seen it in years as he left.

We're not who we were without you, Mama. But maybe we're gonna be okay after all.

Scarlett glanced out toward Ian as he stood, straight and tall, in the dining room, listening to what was probably yet one more person expecting him to perform miracles in some way. He was the go-to man in Sweetgrass, the mayor who refused to accept a title but performed the work nonetheless. If Nana was the heart of Sweetgrass, Ian was its protector. Its get-it-done man. Everyone knew that he would not rest until a problem was fixed, and it was part of his power that he cared nothing for status or position. Ian didn't posture or need acclaim; he needed things to get done. Needed to solve problems.

He saw her looking and cast her a grin and a wink. His eyebrows rose as if to ask *do you need me in there?*

She shook her head, then smiled and blew him a kiss. She hadn't had a champion all that long, but it was certainly nice, knowing she could have one at any given moment. All she had to do was say the word, and Ian would charge in on his white horse.

That she seldom asked bothered him more than a bit at times, she was almost positive.

The warmth in his beautiful brown eyes melted her defenses. Yes, he was overprotective, but after a lifetime of being nearly alone but for a mother who flitted from man to man to man, experiencing Ian's fierce guarding felt like luxury of the highest order.

She blew him a second kiss as Jackson entered.

"Did you need something, Scarlett?"

Oh, this was hard. "I do." She resisted the urge to wring her hands. "I'm not sure how to say this, but…I'm really sorry, Jackson. I don't think I can do all that I wanted to with your initial visits from your staff. I just—" She swallowed. "I'm not used to saying I can't do something. I hate this."

He took her hand. "It's okay. Really."

"But you were counting on me, and now I still don't have the courthouse open and running, and you invested so much—"

He was grinning at her.

"What?"

"You are so much like Aunt Ruby." A fond smile as he delivered the supreme compliment.

But she couldn't accept it. "No, I'm not. I'm not accustomed to failing, Jackson. I never make a promise, then not deliver."

"You're pregnant."

"So?" Everything in her took umbrage. "Women accomplish lots of things despite being pregnant. Life doesn't stop."

"Best I can tell, you're still outworking nine-tenths of the population. So you're not superwoman. Deal with it."

"But—"

He laughed, but the laughter had a hollow ring to it.

Abruptly she noticed how exhausted he seemed.

And dispirited.

"Are you okay? Something's wrong."

"Nothing's wrong." The tone was hollow. At last he sighed. "It's going to work out. I hope."

"Are you having trouble with your employees over this plan to move to Sweetgrass?"

"What? No—well, yeah, but my business is based on the internet. With the cell tower coming online, proximity isn't a huge issue. Sure, I'd prefer that my staff would see what I love about Sweetgrass, but most of them are quite young." He smiled. "Although what the difference in working twenty hours a day in the office in Seattle or here is, I'm not sure."

"But when they do poke their heads out, the nightlife is about as different as humanly possible. And not a Starbucks in sight."

"Yeah. That." Again his gaze went distant. After a moment, he shook himself. Looked at her. "I'm thinking that the community Christmas will work well as a way to introduce a few of them to the essence of Sweetgrass, so don't worry. Truly."

"Spritz them with Eau de Sweetgrass Springs."

His lips curved. "Something like that. I'll figure this out." He sobered. "Scarlett, I wanted to invest in the courthouse and Ruby's Dream because of Aunt Ruby and Ian and you, but not at the expense of your health or your baby's. I truly have no emotional investment in when it comes to fruition or what form it takes. I trust you. Take that worry off your list, all right?" He cocked his head. "I do want to ask, though, if it's possible that some catering could be done down the road, if I needed that. For instance, I'm making plans with Bridger to renovate the old hardware store and the dry goods next door. Make the downstairs office space and the upstairs a set of studios. But because my people tend to work odd hours and long ones, I'd like to promise some sort of commissary for the times when the diner isn't open, and I also wonder if you'd be willing to think about expanding the menu here when you are open." His eyes twinkled. "I do have more than my share of food issues to deal with. Can you do Asian and vegan, for instance? Gluten free?"

"I can do anything. Tell me what you're thinking about."

For a few minutes they discussed options that would allow him to accommodate the more exotic fare his crew was used to consuming.

Scarlett started getting enthused about the possibilities. She could use the kitchen at the courthouse to serve his commissary, and maybe she'd open for dinner at Ruby's Dream on weekend nights only, when Nana could be closed at the diner....

"I can see that brain clicking. I wasn't trying to double your workload but to relieve some of it. Anyway, I honestly don't know how many will choose to relocate. Probably more of them will want to telecommute, but we might stage regular in-person meetings here, sort of retreats. I'm still thinking," he said. "Mostly I just want not to be traveling so much. I want to stay here with my family." But his fond look slid to sad.

"I'm a good listener if you wanted to talk over whatever's bothering you," she prompted.

"I don't doubt it for a minute. I just—marrying into

an existing family is a little more complicated than I realized."

"The kids adore you."

"The girls do. They can't wait."

"But not Ben?"

Jackson heaved a sigh. "I don't want to be angry with Vee for not telling me about him, and I don't want him to be, either. I know it's my fault for leaving and never getting in touch, but—" He shook his head. "We'll figure it out."

"But meanwhile the clock is ticking on a wedding."

"Yeah. And that's on me, too. I pushed Vee into it."

"She loves you, Jackson. Anyone can see that."

Those electric blue eyes locked on hers. "She's the dream I could never forget, however little I believed I'd ever have a chance with her again. We had so many plans when we were young, but then…"

"Life likes to toy with us, doesn't it? Fate has a nasty sense of humor."

"Fate or human error. I've made more than my share of mistakes." He shook it off and straightened. "Thank you, Scarlett. I'm really glad Ian found you. He's the best."

"He is." She had to grin. "Even if he's a wee bit too protective."

"You're a treasure. We dragons like to guard ours." He clasped her shoulder. "Don't spend one more second worrying about the courthouse or the restaurant, all right?" His glance dropped to her belly, then back up. "Take care of that little one. Nothing matters more. We're good at what we do, cousin, but we're not so great at kicking back and going with the flow, are we?"

"Nope."

"Maybe we should form a support group." His handsome face smiled.

She rose to her toes and hugged him. "I'm so glad you came home."

His arms tightened on her. "Me, too. More than I know how to say."

As he drew away, she spoke once more. "If I can do anything…"

He nodded with a smile and walked back into the dining room, where Melba promptly snagged him.

Poor guy.

Better him than me, though.

The more boxes she opened, the more Penny found their family's past springing to life. It hurt and it filled her heart and she couldn't stand it, but she couldn't stop—

"It looks like a fabric bomb went off, and you're the only survivor." Rissa emerged from the stairs, cookies in her hand.

"You were so cute in this dress, Clary—" She extended a scrap of plaid that she recalled a gap-toothed redheaded moppet wearing for her school picture.

"I hated wearing dresses. You're the one who loved prissing around."

"You were the cutest thing in this, your front teeth

missing, grinning at the camera. Funny how you don't look like a pint-sized demon."

"Surely you're not saying I was." Rissa grinned and extended a cookie. "Here."

Penny took it and bit in. "Oh. Oh, wow—I forgot to eat lunch, I just realized." She made short work of the snack and reached out. "More. Gimme."

"What makes you think I brought more than one for you?"

"You did, you know it." But as she glanced around, the cookie stuck in her throat. "Did you know all this was here?"

"Nope. Didn't want to. I was too mad—at all of you. Mama most because she left me, but—"

"I left you, too. Jackson and I both did. There's no way to apologize enough."

"You got that right." Rissa blew out a breath. "But we're moving on now, right? I did promise to forgive you. Even if I still don't want to," she grumbled.

Penny bit her lip. "You deserve to hate me, Clary—Rissa. You do. Mama would have wanted me to take better care of you."

Rissa lifted one shoulder. "I turned out okay."

"More than okay, little sis. You did an amazing job of raising yourself. I'm known for being a strong woman, but I'm peanuts compared to you."

A little girl's eyes peered out of Rissa's bravado. "Thank you." She tried to smile, but it wasn't steady.

"I feel awful," Penny whispered. "I look around at this, and I think of the tremendous love Mama poured into us. She'd be so upset to know that the family she spent her life building and nurturing fell apart without her. She raised me to be better than that." It was her deepest shame and sorrow. She rose to her knees and seized her sister in a hug. "If I could do it over, I would."

Rissa grabbed on and held her tightly. "Just these few months of being someone's mother…I don't know how she did it. We were unbelievably lucky to have her. I don't know anyone who had anything comparable." She released Penny. "But remember what she also said, over and over? Life takes turns you don't expect, but if you like where you are, you can't regret the road that got you there." She gripped Penny's hand. "You're back and Jackson's back, and we all have love in our lives. Dad and Jackson have reconciled. We're strong and united now, even if we weren't always. We are what she raised us to be, at last. Even if she might not like how we got here, I think she'd approve, don't you?"

Penny nodded. "I miss her so much."

"This—" Rissa gestured around them "—has to make it worse. What are you doing?"

Penny explained about the quilt. "Will you help me pick some fabrics that represent all of us?"

"Sure. Any more boxes to open?"

"I've barely made a dent."

Rissa glanced around. Saw a trunk. "Oh, Penny. Remember that? It's Mama's hope chest."

Penny gasped. "Oh! I remember her letting us go through it when—" She gasped. "Do you suppose her wedding dress is still in there?"

Rissa's eyes widened. "Let's see." She picked her way over and opened the trunk. Drew out a zippered bag

Penny remembered as though it was yesterday.

Hastily she joined her sister. With trembling fingers, they opened the bag and let the dress spill out of its second protective wrapping.

"Oh! Oh, Ris…look. It's so beautiful." Lace bodice with camisole beneath, long, flowing chiffon skirt, the dress was fairy princess lovely.

"You should wear it," Rissa said. "When you and Bridger get married." Naked longing was on her features. She and Mackey had done a quick justice of the peace wedding to be eligible to adopt Eric.

There was nothing that appealed more, but—"You and I both grew too big. We're much too tall."

A thought struck her.

Rissa spoke at the same time. "Veronica."

They traded smiles. "Mama would love that," she said.

"Veronica might not want it. And Jackson is eager to spend a fortune on her."

"I don't think that's what she wants, though." Excitement seized Penny, and she wiped away the tears from her sister's eyes, then her own. "She should have the opportunity. But no pressure. We'd better catch Jeanette quickly, though, before she does any work on a new one."

"I'll call her. Then we should go see Veronica."

Penny hesitated. "I…I'm not sure it's a good time."

"Why do you say that? Is something wrong?" Rissa read her expression. "Penny, I'm not the little girl anymore. If there's a problem with my family, I deserve to know. I always hated it that you and Jackson shared everything and left me out."

She was right. They'd been so smug in their twin-hood. "We were wrong to do that. It's more that I'm not sure I'm not imagining things."

"What things?"

"I really don't know. It's just this sense…there was a tension between them at the meeting earlier…or a sadness or…I'm not sure. You didn't notice anything?"

"Not really."

"I hope I'm wrong."

"You used to be infallible when it came to Jackson—and vice versa."

"We'll pay closer attention, okay? Meanwhile, why don't you hang the garment bag over the bannister while we pick out some fabrics and reseal these boxes. We'll call Jeanette as we head to Veronica's."

As they closed up the attic, Penny turned to her sister. "We have to ask Daddy before we do anything."

"Yeah. You're right." Rissa grimaced. "Is he gonna go ballistic?"

"No idea, but we can't do this behind his back." She called out to him from the kitchen door. "Daddy, could you come here for a minute, please?"

He waved to her, spoke to Mackey and headed their way.

Penny could feel her sister's nerves as much as her own as they waited for their father to join them.

"What's up? I was about to take Eric and Samantha—" He took in their serious expressions. "What's wrong?"

Rissa lifted the bag she was holding. "We found something, and we need to talk to you."

"What is it…" As his voice trailed off, they could see the quick flash of grief. "What do you have there?"

"Mama's wedding dress, Daddy."

He went very still. "Where did you find it?"

"It was in the attic. In her hope chest."

He remained frozen as though something terrible might leap from the bag. "What did you want to talk about?"

"We'd like to offer it to Veronica to wear when she marries Jackson. How would you feel about that?"

A tremor ran through him. "I haven't seen it since…" He looked at one, then the other. "She was saving it for you girls."

"She couldn't have known back then that we'd both get so tall. It won't fit either of us, Daddy, but it might fit Veronica."

His look was stricken, his eyes dark and fathomless.

"Do you not want us to offer it?" Rissa asked.

"I—" He turned away. Walked out of the room.

They traded glances. What now?

Then they heard his footsteps returning. He had something in his hand. Extended it. "She was the most beautiful thing I ever saw." His voice was hoarse.

Rissa took it and held the photo between them.

"I haven't seen this in years," Penny whispered. "Oh, Mama…" She lifted her gaze. "She was a beautiful bride."

"Beautiful woman, inside and out," he corrected gruffly.

"She was." Penny could barely speak for the longing that rose in her to see her mother just one more time. To hear her voice. But her father still suffered, so she tried for a distraction. "Jackson looks so much like you did back then."

He shrugged but didn't speak.

Her father had been having fun with Eric, and she'd brought this heartache roaring back. When she could trust her voice again, she met his gaze. "We don't want to hurt you. If you'd rather we put it back, we will. Veronica will never know, or Jackson either."

Powerful emotions battled in his features. At last he exhaled. "No. That would be wrong. Your mama would be real pleased." He shrugged. "'Course it's probably too old-fashioned for a modern woman."

"Veronica's an old-fashioned girl, don't you think?" Rissa asked.

"She's a good one. Boy couldn't do better, that's for sure. She reminds me of your mama in some ways."

And they didn't, Penny thought.

"But not as much as you two."

Her head whipped up, and she noted Rissa's matching astonishment. "I'm nothing like her," Rissa said sadly.

"You are so. You've got her guts and her determination. Her love of this land."

It was true, Penny realized.

"And you, missy. You've got her creativity and her

way with people. Even if you're scared to let them in."

Her vision blurred.

Her father wasn't a hugger, but he pulled a handkerchief from his pocket and handed it over.

Penny took it with a smile, then shared with her sister. "Want to come with us? We're going to take it over right now, if you're sure you're okay with it."

"I am. My Mary wasn't one for sticking stuff up on a shelf. She liked sharing whatever she had, and she would have been pleased as punch to welcome Veronica to the family, you know she would."

They both nodded. "But you don't want to come?"

"Nope. That's women's territory. But you give her my best, would you? And tell her it's okay if she doesn't want it. She'll make a pretty bride, no matter what she wears." The idea was obviously growing on him, though, and his expression was wistful.

He might not be a hugger, and she wasn't either, really, but—"I love you, Daddy." Penny threw her arms around his shoulders.

He startled at first, then returned the hug.

And, to Rissa's astonishment, held out his other arm to her sister. "Get on over here, girl."

For a long, precious moment, years after they would have given nearly anything for a chance like this, the sisters' eyes met, and they snuggled into their father's embrace.

"The kids will be home from school," Rissa pointed out as they drove. "And she'll be busy making supper."

"But they have so little time to put this together. This dress might help." They'd looked it over carefully. There were no moth holes, and Jeanette had said she'd help them get the wrinkles out and alter whatever was needed.

"It's a very old-school dress. Not grand at all, as I imagine Jackson's picturing for her."

"Didn't you think she looked uncomfortable that everyone else was making plans for her wedding?"

"She did, now that you mention it," Rissa acknowledged. "Sweetgrass can get a little overbearing."

"Veronica needs her sisters now." She glanced over and grinned. "A couple of Amazons just might come in handy."

Rissa snorted, but she was smiling. "You can't fight in stilettos."

"Oh, girl, you've never seen me in court. I'm lethal."

As they drove through town on the way to the Butler place, she saw that Jackson's Range Rover was still on the square. "Good," she murmured. "Don't come home yet, big brother."

"Oh, you have got to be kidding." Disgust and dismay vibrated in Rissa's tone. "No way. No freaking way."

"What?" Penny's head whipped in the direction Rissa was pointing. Her mouth dropped open. "Hayley?"

"It better not be Mackey who called her, or that man will not be getting any for the foreseeable future."

"He doesn't have a death wish, Ris." But she was grinning. "She's not that bad."

"You're kidding, right? What do you imagine Scarlett's saying right now? And just you wait—give Barbie a few days, and you tell me how happy you are when you hear those blasted slut shoes clacking and hear that cooing little voice *Oh, Bridger, you're just soooo strong. Let me see those muscles again, big boy.*"

Penny couldn't help herself. She burst out laughing.

Rissa cut her a death ray glare. "Oh, yeah, chuckle away, big sister. We'll see who's laughing in a couple of days."

"You could wipe the floor with her, Cousin Crankypants."

"And don't think I won't," Rissa muttered as she drove them out of town.

Chapter Five

Veronica's doorbell rang.

"I'll get it!" Abby cried, jumping down from the kitchen bar.

"Hold up there," Veronica said. "What do you say?"

Abby's smile was all sunshine. "May I be excused, please?" So perfectly certain of the answer.

Veronica chuckled. "You may. And thank you." She glanced over at Beth. "I wonder who it is?"

"Maybe it's Santa Claus. He might be checking to see who lives here."

Those sweet, hopeful eyes. "Or how good the children have been?"

Beth rolled her eyes. "I've been good, Mommy. We all have. Especially Boo."

The boxer/retriever/mutt mix thumped his tail at the mention of his name.

Or in hopes of being slipped another cookie, more likely.

"I'm on to you, buddy. You know you shouldn't eat people food, right?" She bent to the old hound and cooed. "Who's the best dog, huh?"

More thumps of the tail.

Beth giggled. "I wish Boo could talk, Mommy."

"He does, in his own way, don't you, boy?" She scratched him behind the ears and Boo heaved a doggy moan.

"Mommy, it's Rissa and her sister! Prince Daddy's sister's other sister!"

Veronica looked up. They were bearing a garment bag.

"Sounds like wicked stepsister to me," Rissa remarked.

"Bite me," Penny said. "Hi, Veronica. Sorry to just drop in. Do you have a minute?"

"Want a cookie, Aunt Penny? You're going to be my Aunt Penny, right? As soon as we marry Prince Daddy and we get to be Gallaghers?"

Penny's smile widened. "Wow. You didn't take a single breath in all that, did you?"

"I can talk for a long time," Abby maintained.

"I see that. We're gonna get along just fine, girlfriend." Penny held out a hand for high five.

Abby jumped and slapped her palm against Penny's.

"Okay, wait. I have to ask this first: do you love shoes? And you?" She glanced at Beth. "This is important. Think carefully before you answer." But she was grinning.

"I love shoes!" Abby shouted.

Penny approached Beth. "I'll still love you if you don't have a shoe thing. It's okay."

Slowly Beth extended her foot. Where Abby's sneakers were screaming yellow with lights, Beth had woven little flowers into the shoelaces of her less lurid pink ones.

"Wow. I'm impressed. You did that?" Penny pointed to the flowers.

Beth nodded, eyes huge.

"That calls for a Gallagher hip-bump." Penny gently swiveled her hip to touch Beth's up on the bar stool.

Beth giggled.

"But mine are yellow, Aunt Penny! Like sunshine!"

"And beautifully yellow, I might add." Penny high-fived her again. "So...we're eating cookies and nobody told me?" She jammed one fist on her hip. "Rule number one, right, Ris? Gallagher girls never hoard their chocolate from other Gallagher girls. Oatmeal cookies...no loss. Peanut butter...I can live with that. But chocolate? Oh no. Nonononono," She waggled a finger. "Big, *big* mistake."

"Do you have any chocolate to share?" Beth asked, cookie extended.

Penny leaned in and took a bite. "Not on me, so thank you. I was going to die if I had to wait five more minutes for some. My hero." She leaned toward Abby. "Just between us Gallagher girls—"

"We're not Gallaghers yet," Abby noted. "Not until we marry Prince Daddy and he adopts us."

"Which he will. Because he's not crazy."

Veronica couldn't help stiffening.

Penny's eyes caught hers, and Veronica shook her head faintly, then glanced at Rissa, who frowned.

Penny quickly distracted the girls. "I might or might not have a stash of chocolate at my house. And you might or might not need to come see us so you could check. To practice being Gallaghers, of course."

"Might!" Abby shrieked.

"I would like to come see you," Beth said politely while her sister jumped around, insanely over-excited.

Veronica cleared her throat. "Abby, you need to finish your snack and get started on homework. Beth, are you done?"

"Yes, Mommy." Beth slid down, grabbed her plate and brought it around to the sink. She returned to retrieve her glass and did the same.

Rissa's eyebrows rose, as did Penny's.

"Nice manners, Beth."

"Thank you."

"I have good manners, too," Abby insisted, with a cookie crammed in her mouth and one shoelace untied.

Veronica held her breath as Abby juggled both plate and glass in her small hands.

"Do we—" Abby coughed around her cookie.

"Finish your cookie, young lady, before you speak."

Abby all but inhaled the remainder. Then swallowed. "Done! But Mommy, what's in the bag?"

Veronica met their gazes.

Both Penny and Rissa hesitated.

"I think it's an adult conversation first, girls. Then maybe I can tell you later. Now go upstairs and get to work. Chop chop."

"Ookay," Abby sighed heavily, then stopped in front of Rissa. "You won't leave before we're done, will you?"

Rissa glanced at Veronica. "Um…"

"They'll wait for you to say goodbye if they need to leave before you're done. Now shoo."

With a martyr's sagging shoulders, Abby left the room. Behind her, Beth stopped between Jackson's sisters. "If I'm a Gallagher, do I get to be tall like you?"

"Excellent question, kiddo," Rissa said. "Scarlett's a Gallagher, you know. So is Aunt Ruby."

"But they're short. Really short."

"They are. But we still like them, right?"

Beth nodded solemnly.

"We'll probably like each other fine, even if some of us wind up tall or short."

Seemingly satisfied, Beth smiled and left the room.

"They're awesome," Rissa said.

Veronica couldn't disagree. "Thank you. So what's up?"

Penny cleared her throat. "Well, this is just an idea, and you are absolutely welcome to say no, but...we might have a dress for you—only if you want it. You don't have to, but it's closer to your size and—"

"Where did you get it?"

Rissa held up the bag. "We just found it. I've never gone through what's in the attic before. It's still wrinkled and you might not—"

Veronica's breath caught. Her eyes filled. "Is it your mother's?" she whispered.

"Yes."

She had adored Jackson's mother. Mary Gallagher had been so much more a mother to her than her own had ever been. "I loved your mother." She caught Penny's eye. "But don't you want to wear it?"

"I would give a lot to be able to, but as I'm sure you recall, Mama was much closer to your size than mine."

Penny bit her lip. "I don't want you to feel pressured, but I think Mama would be very pleased if you did decide you like it. But honestly, it's okay if you don't."

"What about Jeanette?"

"We already called her as soon as we found this. She's fine with it. She said she could help alter it—but seriously, you don't have to if you'd rather have what Jackson could buy you or—"

Veronica's heart was beating double-time. She was afraid to want this, but somehow wearing Mary's dress would be so much more like the wedding she would have wished for, all those years ago.

"Let's go in my room, in case the girls come down. I'd rather not have anyone know yet. I'd want Jackson to have his say, though, before any decision is made. He might not be comfortable with this."

"I'm pretty sure my brother wants you to be happy, whatever that means. But yes, absolutely, he should weigh in. Lead the way," Penny said.

Rissa pushed the bedroom door closed, and Veronica clasped her hands together. "I'm terrified."

"Let's do it," Rissa said, and began unzipping the bag. When she drew out the dress, Veronica gasped.

Mary's dress was...perfect. Fitted lace top with cap sleeves and a sweetheart neckline. A chiffon skirt, several layers of it that softly fell to a scalloped lace hem. A flat satin bow at the waist.

Simple. Feminine. Stunning.

Her vision blurred as she looked at the sisters. "It's so beautiful. It's exactly what I wanted without ever realizing...are you sure? She would want you—"

Rissa never cried, and Penny was reputed to be a shark.

Yet in this moment, all of them had tears in their eyes, and the moment felt almost…holy.

Veronica clasped her hands in front of her mouth until she could find her voice. "I'm scared to death to try it on, I want it so badly. I know Jackson is willing to buy me the world, but I don't want Paris or New York." She tore her gaze from the gorgeous dress. "David and I eloped and got married by a JP in San Antonio and it was okay because we weren't marrying for love. It was all I could do not to fall on the floor and weep because I wanted to be marrying Jackson, not David. I don't know how David dealt with me. I wept through our wedding night and for months afterward, I was a zombie…" She bit her lip. "But he stuck with me, and he loved me until I could love him. He gave me two beautiful girls, and he took Ben as his own." She lifted her gaze to the two women. "I am such a mess over this. I didn't expect to feel this guilty. I thought I was past the grieving and mostly I am, but—" She wrestled her voice under control. "Jackson deserves so much better. How can I be this messed up when I'm finally getting to be with the love of my life? I'm sorry—I'm sorry. He's your brother and—"

She buried her faced in her hands and whirled away. "I'm so embarrassed."

Then there they were, one to each side. Penny drew her close and let her sob on her shoulder, while Rissa patted her back. "You're not alone anymore, Veronica," Penny murmured. "Not ever again. You have a family.

All of you do."

Oh, the relief of it, the breathless wonder…the unimaginable luxury. She and Tank had been alone to face their childhood, each in their own way, and they'd never been close, but her brother had tried to shield her from the violence always lurking, threatening to explode.

David had been aware of the artificiality of their joining. She'd done everything she could to overcome their rocky start and they'd built a life together, but then David, too, had been snatched away. She'd dug in, squared her shoulders and pushed on through days and months when she could barely breathe around the pain of losing him, the shock, the terror of how she'd manage to keep body and soul together for all of them.

And now…

She had a chance at her dream—if only she could make peace with her past.

She straightened. Drew in a jagged breath. Scrubbed at her face. Rissa turned away and found a tissue box, handed them around.

"Don't even think you've finished crying until you've heard the bad news."

"What?" Veronica's heart seized.

"Hayley's back in town," Rissa pronounced in tones of doom.

Relief swamped her.

They broke up laughing.

It felt…amazing.

They sniffed and blew their noses and wiped their eyes…and giggled.

She felt reborn. "Okay." She heaved a breath. "Okay,

let's do this."

"Strip 'em," Penny ordered.

"Um…"

"Oh, don't tell me you're modest. Sorry, but you're in our wheelhouse now, the sister zone. You don't have anything we haven't seen."

"Except mine are better," Rissa intoned.

Penny snickered. "You think that."

As the two bantered, Veronica managed to take off her blouse and jeans and resisted the urge to cover herself.

A whole new world indeed.

Then the dress was being lowered over her head, and she wanted to turn to look in the mirror, but Penny wouldn't let her. "Not until I've got you fastened up."

"Is it going to—"

But Veronica could already feel that it fit.

"It's as if it was made for you, I swear. You're going to need probably three-inch heels, since this can't be hemmed with that lace around the edge, but hey— shopping trip!"

"Kill me now," Rissa groaned.

"Beth and I got this. And Hayley, of course."

Veronica wanted to laugh, but she wanted worse to see. "Now?"

"Almost—okay, yes. Turn around."

Veronica bit into her lower lip as she turned and… "Oh." Her eyes filled again.

She turned from side to side, adoring the swish of the chiffon as it fell so gracefully to the floor. "It really does fit."

"As though it was made for you, for real," Rissa agreed.

Veronica glanced over at Penny. "You're not that much taller than me."

Penny snorted. "Yeah, only about seven inches. Before heels."

"I just feel bad…"

"Don't." Penny touched her arm. "Seriously. If you don't have one from your mother you'd rather wear—"

"No." Her mother had been a sad excuse for a parent, a wraith who was too terrified of her husband to care for her children. "No. Not even if I did." She couldn't bear thinking of her mother in the same breath as Mary Gallagher. "It would be an unbelievable honor. I mean, I would love this gown even if it hadn't belonged to Mary, but that it did…I can't tell you what this means. If you're sure."

The sisters glanced at each other and clasped hands. "Positive."

She summoned a wobbly smile. "It definitely meets Abby's princess dress qualification." She smoothed the skirt. "I know it's not mine, but I don't want to take it off."

"Then don't. Well, at least until Jackson gets home."

"I wonder who made it," Veronica asked.

"I think Mama had a hand in the design and probably helped, but I'm guessing her mother did. We can ask Aunt Ruby."

A quick knock on the door made it swing open. "Mom, I need to talk to you for a sec—"

Veronica froze.

"Sorry, the door wasn't latched—" Ben went stock still.

Veronica found herself unable to speak at his stricken look.

"Doesn't your mother look gorgeous?" Penny asked. "It was your grandmother's wedding dress—

Ben didn't say a word, only met his mother's shocked gaze with his own. Something dark and hurt rippled through his eyes.

He turned and fled.

Leaving a stunned silence behind him.

Suddenly Veronica couldn't get out of the gown quickly enough. "I have to talk to him. Please—help me—"

"Sure. I'm sorry. Maybe we shouldn't have—"

"Vee?" Jackson's voice came from down the hall.

"I'll get the door." Rissa raced over and locked it.

Veronica's thoughts scrambled. Her fingers were clumsy, and she was terrified of harming the gown.

But more terrified of hurting her son.

"Don't come in, Jackson," Penny shouted.

"What's going on? Ben raced past me without a word, and the bedroom door is locked—"

It was all Veronica could do to be careful enough as she raced to get out of the dress and into her clothes. "I'm sorry. I should hang it up, but—" Every cell of her vibrated with the need to follow her child. "I have to talk to Ben."

"We've got this," Rissa reassured. "Could we help?"

"Thank you, but no. This is my mess to fix." Dressed, she yanked open the door and vaulted past a gaping Jackson. "Don't go in that room," she shouted at him as she tore out after her child.

Jackson started after her, then glanced back at his sisters. "Where are the girls?"

"Upstairs, doing homework," Rissa said.

"Will you stay with them?"

"Of course."

"What the hell happened?"

He could barely make himself linger long enough for Penny to answer. "She was trying on a wedding dress. Ben saw her and freaked. Took off."

He swore, then nodded and charged off in pursuit. Loped out the back door.

Ben was climbing the rise to David's grave.

Veronica was scrambling after. "Ben, please. Talk to me."

"Leave me alone, Mom!" he shouted.

Jackson caught up with her quickly.

She looked…wrecked. "I have to talk to him."

Jackson nodded. "I'll go with you."

She started to shake her head but halted. "It should be me."

"I'm the problem, Vee. You and he were fine be-fore."

Tears spilled over her lashes. "It's not your fault, it's mine."

He reached for her hand. Closed it inside his. "We're

in this together. I won't try to stop you, but I should be there if we're ever to have any hope of being a family."

Her lips pressed together, and he could see her swallow. "All right." Chin lifted, shoulders resolute, she began to climb again.

But her hand trembled in his.

He closed his other hand around her delicate one. Deceptively so. She might be the strongest woman he'd ever met, as strong as his mother. He lifted their clasped hands to his lips and kissed her ice-cold fingers. "You're not alone anymore, Veronica."

She cast him a grateful, terrified glance.

Then they were at the spot beneath the towering oak where David was buried.

"I don't want to talk to you." Ben's voice shook.

Veronica stepped up beside him. "Then we won't talk."

Jackson took his other side. And said nothing.

But the boy's pain hurt him. Jackson waited. Locked his jaw.

Ben cast him an odd glance, almost pleading.

Jackson had been trying to respect the greater bond of mother and child. Veronica had been with this boy all his life. He didn't want to get between them, but—

He knew how it was to be a young man trying to figure out how to be a grown man.

With no father to help him. Jackson's own had been alive, but he'd cared nothing for Jackson. Had loathed everything about him at the end.

Jackson cast a glance over at Veronica, who stood so bravely, so fiercely in defense of her child.

Behind Ben's back, he touched her shoulder.

She glanced over.

His next words had better be the best of his life.

"Would you give us a minute, Vee?" Then he asked the more difficult question. "Would you trust me?" He looked into her eyes, those he loved beyond life and death and promises of forever. *I won't hurt him*, he tried to convey with his eyes.

Hers were tremulous. Heartsore.

For the longest moment, time spun out and worlds collided. He was Ben's father by birth, but David had been the man who'd formed Ben. The man who lay in the grave here had proven himself; Jackson had only begun.

At last, she nodded. Turned to her son, hand on his arm. "Ben, I would never hurt you…"

The boy's jaw flexed. "I know, Mom." With visible effort, he faced her. "I'd be an idiot if I didn't know you love me."

She scanned her son's face for the truth, then, at last, nodded. Her gaze switched to Jackson's, visibly pleading.

Jackson reached out and stroked her cheek. *Thank you*, he mouthed.

Then she left them, though Jackson could see the reluctance in every line of her frame.

When Veronica returned to the house, her features were ravaged.

Penny glanced toward the stairs.

"I'll go hang out with them to give you time to talk," Rissa offered. "But I want to know what's going on. I don't want Jackson hurt."

"Me, either. Thanks." Penny went to meet Veronica and led her deeper into the kitchen where they wouldn't be overheard. "What's wrong? Ben doesn't want his mother and father to get married?" She had to work to keep the shock out of her own tone.

"No, it's not that, I don't think." She bit her lip. "But he's hurt Jackson, and I don't know how to fix this."

"I thought they were getting along great now."

"So did we. But then the girls started asking if they were Gallaghers, and Jackson asked if he could adopt them, and then they asked if he'd adopt Ben, too, but—"

"But what? Jackson doesn't need to adopt Ben. He's Jackson's biological child."

"Yes, but... I think Ben is...torn. He didn't answer, and I could see how that hurt Jackson, even though Jackson said it was okay. It wasn't. You could see it in his eyes."

"Why does Ben need to agree? He's Jackson's son."

"David is listed as father on his birth certificate. His legal name is Butler."

Penny hadn't stopped to consider that legalities would be murky. "Jackson has all kinds of lawyers on retainer."

"That's not it. And I understand Ben's hesitation. He's proud of Jackson and is beginning to love him, but..." She exhaled. "David raised him. David was the only father he ever knew. It was wrong of me not to tell him about Jackson, I see now, but…we thought Jackson was never coming back. For all we knew he was dead all these years. David offered to raise Ben as his, and I promised I'd never tell Ben that he wasn't David's child." She looked up. "He is David's son, in so many ways. He may look like Jackson, and he has some of Jackson's skills, but…David made him who he is. Ben loved his fath—David. Looked up to him. So yes, he's torn. He doesn't want to betray David, however illogical that sounds. My first instinct is to insert myself between them to try to keep them from hurting each other—but they'll never form a relationship if I do. I have to trust Jackson with him. Mostly I do, but…Jackson's never been a father. He's trying so hard, and he didn't push Ben on it earlier. He wants Ben to have time to think, but…it hurts him, that hesitation. As it understandably should."

Veronica wrapped her arms around her waist. "It's all my fault. And even though the girls are all for it, they're David's biological children. Do we just erase David as though he never existed? He was a good man, Penny. He doesn't deserve that."

Penny clasped her arm. "He was a very good man. Wow. I'm sorry—I never even thought—"

"Ben's hesitation blindsided Jackson—me, too. And I feel guilty. He wouldn't be running into this if I'd told Ben who his biological father was long before. I handled it all wrong."

"It wasn't all your fault. There were two of you there the night Ben was conceived."

Veronica shook her head. "The accident changed

everything. Jackson would never have left with David's sister Beth that night if he and I hadn't fought."

"But he didn't know you were pregnant."

"I didn't know, either. He couldn't stand how things were with your father any longer. Everything was piling up on him. He wanted to leave, but I wouldn't. I thought he should graduate first. Then we'd leave together."

"What about you? You still had a year of high school to go."

"I would have followed him anywhere. It was our vow. We would leave together. Go back East. Go to college—did you know he'd been admitted to MIT? With a full scholarship?"

"Yes. He told me before he told Daddy."

"He knew your father would be furious, not proud."

Penny shook her head sadly. "It's criminal, how Dad treated him."

"You don't know criminal. My father, what he did to Tank—"

Penny wanted to hear more, but not right now. She was worried for her twin.

Veronica continued. "Your father only wanted his son and heir to follow in his footsteps. He handled it wrong, though."

"He did. It's a relief that they've moved on. They're doing so much better."

"I agree."

"And Dad is over the moon about Ben. We all are. He's amazing, Veronica. You're a wonderful mother."

"I don't feel very wonderful right now. I've created such a mess. I thought the worst was over, but...maybe it will never be." Troubled hazel eyes rose to meet Penny's. "I never loved David the way he deserved to be loved. I did my best, and we were happy, but…it was never the passion I feel for Jackson. Jackson always had this hold on me, and David knew it." She swallowed visibly. "I don't know if I can marry Jackson under these circumstances. And I shouldn't be telling you this. He's your twin."

"But you're my friend. And, I very much hope, my new sister. Look, Jackson doesn't have to have his way on the timing. You can wait."

"We could. But you didn't see his eyes when he asked me. This is the only Christmas gift he wants."

"He's used to getting what he wants. He can buy out half the known universe."

"He hasn't had what his heart longed for, not in all the years since the accident. He's been so alone, Penny. He may have lots of toys, but he hasn't had love. He hasn't had family. He needs that."

"So what will you do?"

"I don't know," Veronica murmured. "I just don't know." She looked up, eyes tormented. "I love them both. How do I choose? I can't. I'm responsible for both their hearts."

Chapter Six

Jackson waited to see if Ben would speak first.

When the boy said nothing, Jackson took a gamble.

He knelt by David's headstone and placed his palm on the grass covering his friend's remains. "I wish you were here, bud."

"No, you don't," Ben retorted. "How could you?"

Jackson shifted his weight back to his heels, then rose. "Do you think I'm glad your father is dead?"

Ben's eyes wavered. "But he's not my—"

"He is, Ben. I wish to hell that wasn't the case, that our lives had played out differently, the way your mother and I always intended, but...we wouldn't have you if all of that changed. And I would never give up knowing you, however much it tears at my gut that I missed so much of your life.

"David is your true father." Jackson forced the words past his throat. "The earliest memory I have of him was about five years old. Ian and I were throwing rocks at a snake, trying to make it use its rattle."

Ben's surprise registered. "That's stupid."

He shrugged. "We were kids. It seemed exciting."

"What did Dad—David do?"

"You can call him Dad. I don't take offense." Even though Jackson had been honored when Ben began calling him that. When confusion rose in Ben's eyes, Jackson returned to the memory. "He told us we were idiots." Jackson grinned. "Then he hunted for a rock and showed us a better way."

A small laugh escaped Ben.

"I loved David. I wish to hell he was still here." He cleared his throat. "Do I want him to have your mother? No. I loved her first." He pinned Ben with his gaze. "But I'd want to win her honestly. Dead is an advantage."

"What?"

He'd just gambled all the marbles, hadn't he? "What I mean is…being dead keeps David from being real. He was a really great guy, but he wasn't perfect. Ever notice how he was fussy with everything needing to be in its proper spot?"

A quick, fond smile. "Yeah."

"Ian was a total slob, since he didn't have a mom. Me, my mom just closed the door to my room when she couldn't stand it. Or threatened to bring in a shovel and toss it out my window."

Ben laughed. "My mom's done that. And my dad—"

"Yeah. Talk about anal." The atmosphere lightened a little with the revelation that they both knew David well.

"He was a really great guy," Jackson finally said. "If I couldn't raise my own child, I'd have chosen him in a heartbeat." He tried to push away his anger. "But I didn't get a choice."

"Mom didn't—"

Jackson held up a hand. "I know. It's my fault. I screwed up. I didn't think I had any alternative but to leave. My father threw me out, told me I wasn't his son anymore. He hated the sight of me."

"He said that?" Ben's tone held outrage.

"Yeah. But in fairness, I didn't make things easy. I broke his heart because I didn't want what he wanted for me. I couldn't wait to grow up and leave Sweetgrass. Your mother and I never planned to stay here. Once she graduated, we didn't intend to come back."

"She told me you had a full ride at MIT."

Jackson shrugged. "Yeah. Listen, you're smart enough, and you won't need a scholarship. Do you know what you want to do about college?"

"I don't know. I didn't think…I mean, after Dad died, there wasn't any money and…"

"There's money now. You can go anywhere you want."

"You said you weren't going to bribe me with games and junk."

"I'm not. Your college money will depend on your grades. You screw around and blow it, and you'll be back here, working in the greenhouse."

"Or coding for you?"

Jackson's heart skipped. "Would you want to?"

"I'm good at it."

"You are. But you still need to get out in the world, see what you really want."

Ben grew silent. "Dad intended me to take over the ranch, but I'm not a Butler."

Jackson's gaze whipped to his. "Of course you are."

"Just because his name is on my birth certificate—"

"No. Because he made you who you are. I didn't get the chance, and it hurts like hell that I didn't, but maybe you wouldn't have turned out this great without him."

Ben looked so uncertain. Jackson longed to embrace his son, but this balance was dicey already…

"You think I'm great?" Ben said in a small voice, his eyes open and vulnerable.

"Of course. Ben, I love you." Jackson threw caution to the winds and gripped Ben's shoulder. "Not because you're my blood—okay, yes, I'm proud as hell that you're mine—but because of who you are. Son, there is no limit to what you can do with your life, and I will be there every step of the way if you'll let me." Jackson squeezed the boy's shoulder but forced himself to go slow.

He let go and exhaled. "But I am not going to force you into any life or try to impose any of my choices. I know what that feels like." He looked straight into his son's eyes. "I would be the proudest man on this earth for you to bear my name, but not if it makes you feel like you're abandoning that very good man who raised you. And what you decide to call me is up to you. Maybe you should just call me Jackson for now, the way you did before we learned I'm your father."

"That seems…disrespectful. I don't know what to do," Ben said after a moment.

Though a part of Jackson wanted his child to choose him, this was about Ben, not him. "I won't lie and say I like it, but I can live with it for now. How about I promise you that I'll speak frankly and you do the same?

Take the time to think about all this until you do know."
He squeezed Ben's shoulder again. "I want to marry your
mother so badly I can't think straight. I want us to be a
family. I have this really primitive urge to lock this all
down, set it in stone. But the fact that I've been alone a
long time is not your problem. You know what I want
more than any of that?"

"What?"

"I want you to be the one to decide how we move
forward. My dad didn't give me that choice. When I was
just a little past your age, he told me it was his way or the
highway. I'm not doing that to you. I want you to be at
peace. If we're all to have a future, I want you to be there
with a whole heart." He pointed to the headstone. "That
man loved your mother long before I left. I knew it, but
no way was I stepping aside because I knew deep in
here—" He pointed a thumb at his chest "—that she
and I belonged together. And we did. We do—but life
isn't often easy or simple. Sometimes it's messy. Sometimes you don't know what to do right that moment."

"So what do you choose? How do you choose?"

"Sometimes you have to be patient, Ben. You have
to dig deep and wait to hear what your heart is really
saying. And you have to think about who you're going to
hurt." He glanced back at the house. "I'm going to marry
your mother, but maybe not as soon as I'd like. She's
torn up over this, and I'm not going to make it worse.
She puts you children first, over the needs of her heart,
and I'm pretty sure that's what my mother did a lot of
the time. Being a mom means your heart is always
divided." He found a smile. "I'm talking to you, man to

man, Ben, and I'm telling you that I won't say I like waiting, but dreams are worth waiting for. My dream is all of us as a family, but the right kind of family, one where everyone feels respected and cherished. So I am going to wait until you're ready to come to this family with an open heart, until you no longer feel torn between David and me. And I promise you this: I will never expect you to forget that good man and what he meant to you. Not ever."

"I don't want to hurt you, Da—" Ben halted. "Jackson." He shook his head. "That sounds wrong now. I don't know what to call you."

"I guess Prince Daddy is out." Given how badly he wanted this boy to claim him fully as his father, Jackson was surprised he could make a jest.

A quick grin from Ben.

"We'll figure it out. This is hard. You miss him, and so does your mom. The girls have it a little easier because they were so young when he died, but they miss him, too. I do myself, but I've had longer to get used to not having him around." Jackson straightened. "We will never forget him, and I want to help you find a way to feel that you honor his life and make peace with his passing as much as any of us can with someone so important to us." He leveled a look filled with all the love he held for this boy. "Just please remember that when you want to talk, I want to listen. You're not alone anymore, Ben. You don't have to be the man of the house, though I'm grateful as hell for all you've done to take care of your mom and the girls. It's okay to be a kid again."

He could almost see the weight of the burdens slide from Ben's shoulders. "I didn't mind."

"You probably did sometimes, but there's no shame in that. Who wouldn't? You're supposed to be chasing girls and playing football." He grinned. "And studying, of course."

Ben looked up. "You're really not mad?"

"I'm really not."

Then Ben moved, and suddenly Jackson's arms were full of boy.

He sighed in relief and held his son close. "We'll figure this out, son."

For a moment, he felt Ben's shoulders shake, then too quickly, the boy stepped back. Swiped at his eyes. "I'd better talk to Mom."

"Want me to?"

Vulnerable. "Would you?"

"Sure. But you might want to give her a hug." Jackson turned. "Ready to go back, or you want to stay here a bit?"

Ben hesitated. "I might stay."

"That's fine. Just fine." Jackson clasped his shoulder, then started down the rise alone.

"Pops?" Ben called out.

Jackson closed his eyes in gratitude. "Yes?"

"Is Pops okay? Would that work?"

He could be Pops. He could be whatever Ben needed him to be. "Pops is just fine."

"Thanks. For understanding, I mean. For letting me think."

Jackson looked back and met his son's gaze. "I love

you, Ben."

Ben nodded. "Mom looks beautiful in that dress."

"Yeah? Think she'll let me see it?"

A quick grin. "What do you think?"

"Yeah," Jackson responded. "Not a chance." He turned and headed down once more. Maybe he wouldn't get the Christmas gift he really wanted, but that was small potatoes in the span of a life.

"Pops?"

"Yes?"

"I'm not sorry I'm your son. I'm proud of that."

Jackson stopped in his tracks. Felt his eyes burn.

And sometimes you got the dream that was much more important.

"Thank you." He cleared his throat. "We'll call when supper's ready."

"Okay."

Jackson entered the back door, looking around for Veronica.

"I'm sorry," Veronica said to Penny before he made it to the kitchen. "I shouldn't have dumped all that on you."

Penny grabbed her arm before she could flee. "You can talk to me anytime you want. I want to help."

"The only thing that will help, I fear, is time. And time is the one thing we don't have, now that everybody's involved." Veronica summoned a smile. "It'll work out somehow."

"Want us to take the girls somewhere?"

Before she could answer, Jackson came to her, tucked her into his side. Kissed her softly, then faced his twin. "Hey, sis."

"Hey." The love between them was tangible. "Are you okay?"

"Yeah."

But he wasn't, Veronica could tell. She was sure Penny could, too.

Fortunately, Penny didn't push him. "How is Ben?" she asked instead.

"He's okay."

"Why isn't he with you?" Veronica asked.

Jackson looked down at her. "He wanted to be with David for a while."

She frowned. "Are you all right with that?"

He framed her face with his hands. "I'm not going to do to him what my dad did to me. I told him to take his time. To figure out what he wants. And what to call me."

"But Christmas is—" She hesitated. Summoned her courage. "I don't feel right about getting married with this unsettled."

"I know." Disappointment flared, but quickly he masked it. "I'm not pushing you into a wedding until you're ready."

"It's not that—"

"It's all right. I understand. And if he doesn't want to change his name, I'm okay with that."

She frowned. "You can't mean that."

"Is it what I want? No. But am I going to play rough

with my child? No way." His smile was tender. "I want to be okay with it, and I will. This has to be his choice." He drew her in, and she absorbed once again the luxury of his strength. His honor. His commitment.

"But what happens about the wedding?"

For a second, his eyes held mischief. "Depends. Can I see the dress? Where did you get it?"

"No, you cannot see it." Rissa entered the room. "You really want to risk jinxing this, after all the years you two have waited to be together?"

"Nope. Put that way, guess not." He shifted his gaze to Veronica. "Ben said you looked beautiful in it."

"He did?" Something inside her eased. "It's your mother's wedding gown."

It wasn't often one could surprise Jackson that much, but he looked gobsmacked. "Seriously?"

"Yes."

"Where on earth—"

"It was in the attic. In pretty good condition. Jeanette says she'll help us steam out the wrinkles. I didn't see anything that needed mending, did you?" Penny asked the other two.

Veronica clung to Jackson's side. "No, but I was a little emotional."

He glanced down. "Do you really want to wear it? You know I'd buy you anything you want."

"I really do," she said. "I adored your mother."

"And the dress looks like it was made for her," Rissa pointed out.

"Penny? You didn't want to wear it?"

"I already asked," Veronica said.

"Jackson," Penny said patiently. "Do you not remember how much shorter Mama was than either Rissa or me?"

"And it couldn't be altered to fit you?"

Worry struck Veronica. "Do you not want me to wear it, Jackson?"

"What? No—of course I do if that's what you—" He gripped her again. "I'd marry you if you were wearing rags, Vee. I don't care what you wear. I just want you to be happy. I want to make your dreams come true."

"You already have," she answered honestly. Then glanced out the back. "If Ben would just be okay with this."

"Us getting married isn't the problem. It's figuring out how to become a Gallagher when he always thought he was a Butler. And I don't want to make him choose. He's my son, whatever his name is."

"But don't you want—"

"Him bearing my name? Hell, yes. But am I going to box him in the way my dad did me? Absolutely not. David was my friend, and obviously he was one hell of a dad. I just hope I can be half as good."

She smiled and laid her hand on his jaw. "You already are." She rested her head against his heart for a minute, and he gathered her close. Even with his sisters watching, she didn't feel self-conscious, really.

They were becoming a family.

Finally, she stepped back. "Well, I need to get supper going. Would you two like to join us?" she asked Rissa and Penny.

"Thanks," Penny said, "But I want to see Bridger."

"Invite him, too, and Mackey." She glanced at Jackson. "And your dad?"

Jackson didn't even hesitate. "Sure. Do we have enough?" He halted. "But wouldn't you rather have the evening for privacy with Ben?"

"My son—our son—does not make hasty decisions, in case you hadn't noticed."

Jackson grimaced. "Unlike his father."

She rose to her toes and kissed his cheek. "Some of your hasty decisions have been wonderful." They shared a moment filled with memories, some of them very sweet.

"Ben and I will talk when he's ready," she said and turned back to the women who had so generously given her a treasure. "Please? We'd love to have you. Eric is included, of course."

Rissa spread her hands. "I'll call Mackey."

"Call Bridger, too, okay?" Penny asked. "I'll help Veronica. You—" She pointed at her sister. "Don't even think about touching the food."

Rissa made a rude gesture, grinning the whole time.

The laughter was a welcome balm, washing away the clouds of emotion that had sent them on a roller coaster ride.

Chapter Seven

Cookie Day dawned bright and early. Ruby and her crew served a buffet breakfast at the diner while Scarlett oversaw the initial setup at the courthouse kitchen.

In between being ordered to sit down by every last person present.

"I love this place, but you all drive me completely nuts," she complained, popping up and down like some demented jack in the box.

"One cookie recipe, I remind you," Penny said, holding up an imperious finger. "One. You can count, right?"

"They only taught about butter and crap in Paris, Sissy," Rissa snickered. "City Girl doesn't do numbers."

Scarlett glared at her. Ian grinned and nodded his thanks. Rissa snickered. "You'll get your turn. For right now, sit down or we'll send you home."

"It's Cookie Day," Scarlett pouted, crossing her arms over her chest. "I'm a Gallagher, just like you."

"We're all Gallaghers today, Cousin Scarlett," chimed Eric. "But in school they tell us it's important to be polite and wait our turn. Right, Mom?"

Rissa grinned proudly and gave her son a thumbs-up.

Mackey clapped him on the shoulder. "Good one, son."

The door opened, and in trooped Jackson, Veronica and the girls.

"Good morning. Where's Ben?" Penny asked.

"Outside with Bridger," Jackson responded, "Learning Barbecue 101. They're practicing for the Community Christmas."

"I was thinking cookies for lunch," Scarlett protested.

"You have a baby to grow. Can't do that on cookies," Ian reminded her.

"I know that. I ate."

"Not enough." He crouched before her, clearly worried. "Anything I can bring you to help out?"

"Coffee," she whimpered.

"So sorry. Seriously. I'll get you some decaf."

"Not the same..." She sighed dramatically. "Thank you," she said to him, stroking his face. "For putting up with me, taking care of me. Not strangling me in my sleep."

Ian rose on his knees and pulled her toward him. "No problem. It's this love thing. Can't help myself."

She dropped her head to his shoulder and whimpered. "I want this baby so much, but dang..."

Ian's face split in a wide grin. He winked over her shoulder at Rissa. "She said *dang*. She's a real Texan now. I won't have to teach our baby two languages."

As the group chuckled, he gathered her in and rocked side to side. She burrowed closer. "Sure you're okay being here? I could take you home. Put you back to bed."

"Will you come with me?" she spoke into his neck. And wriggled against his body.

His eyebrows rose nearly to his hairline. "Well, now." A grin as wide as the horizon. "Penny, I think I'd better—"

"Yeah, yeah, yeah…it's Cookie Day. You can do that anytime."

Half the heads in the room whipped in her direction.

Bridger had just walked in, and faces turned in his direction. "What?" he asked.

"Dude, this is not a good sign. Your woman thinks there's something more important than s—oof!" Mackey took an elbow in the belly from Rissa. She pointed to the kids in the room.

"Than what, Uncle Mackey?" asked Abby.

"Than, uh…"

"Than sarsaparilla. Or sopapillas, maybe," contributed Arnie. "I'm old, so I don't hear real well. What kind of cookies are you making, Miss Abby?"

The kids switched gears on a dime as they took turns calling out the cookie recipe they intended to make.

It was going to be a long day, Penny thought.

A deep voice spoke behind her as a kiss landed on her nape. "Did I do such a poor job this morning you've forgotten already?"

She grinned over her shoulder at Bridger, surprised to discover she could still blush. "That thing you did?" She kept her voice soft. "With the bath gel?" She fanned herself a little. "Not hardly. I only meant—"

Her mouth was seized in a hot, hard kiss that softened to sweetness. She turned in his arms, ignoring the jeers and cheers coming from behind them.

And she felt once more the sting of what she was denying him.

She wasn't sure what she was waiting for. There was no question she wanted this man for the rest of her life. She couldn't imagine loving anyone more.

"Uh-oh. I really am falling down on the job if you can still think while I'm kissing you."

"You don't know what I'm thinking," she protested.

"What? No. But that you are? Oh, yeah." He drew back. "You okay?"

She didn't know what to do with her confusion, but she was not marring this day he'd been looking forward to as much as the kids. She cradled his strong jaws in her hands. "How could I not be, looking at this face?" She slid her arms around his neck and kissed him with all the love she felt for this remarkable, generous man who was so much better at love than she feared she would ever be.

He picked her up and began walking toward the door.

She laughed against his lips. "Bridger, stop that!"

Around them fond laughter arose.

She smacked his shoulder. "Put me down. I'm working."

"Break time," he said. "Carry on, people. She'll be back."

And he carted her outside as, once out of the view of the children, she hitched her legs around his waist.

Back inside, Jackson drew Veronica into his side

while Mackey wrapped his arms around Rissa's waist. Ian picked Scarlett up and replaced her in the chair, holding her on his lap.

Click-clack click-clack.

A growl rose from Rissa's throat. Scarlett groaned.

"Hey, Hayley," greeted Mackey. "You here to make cookies?"

A few minutes later, Penny returned without Bridger, her color high, her hair in disarray. When everyone looked at her, she merely lifted a smug eyebrow.

Then she spotted the newcomer. "Fab shoes, Hayley."

The little blonde preened. Then her gaze dropped to Penny's feet. "Yours, too—oh."

Penny looked down and realized just how far she'd gone native.

"You should see my red cowboy hat to match." She turned to go to her former station.

Ben stepped in her path. "Aunt Penny?"

"Hey, Ben. Great to have you here."

"As if I could miss." But he didn't seem too worked up over it. "Can I talk to you for a minute?"

"Sure. What's up?"

"Not here." His voice was barely a whisper.

"Oh. Sure." She thought for a second, then spoke louder. "Ben and I are going to see if Aunt Ruby needs anything."

Once outside, she walked the long way around the courthouse. "What can I help you with?"

"Is it too late?"

"For what?"

"For Mom to marry Pops for Christmas."

She studied him. "Does that mean you're okay with it?"

"I was always okay with my parents getting married." He shrugged. "A blind man could see how much they love each other. It was just—"

"The adoption thing."

"Yeah." He paused. "I mean, I know it was stupid, since I'm his real son, but—"

"But David was your father. He raised you."

"Yeah. And it seems kinda disloyal to ditch his name."

"Do you have to?"

"That's what I was wondering. What if I just added Gallagher, and Butler stayed in my name, just not my last name?"

"Hey, you could be like royalty. They have a whole string of names. That's what you mean? Keep your full Benjamin Edward Butler and add Gallagher?"

"That's lame, right? I should ditch my middle name, but it's my, well, Edward Butler wasn't my real great-grandfather, but—"

"David's grandfather was a kind man. Names are important, and yours should feel right to you. That's your choice to make, and I know your folks would agree. You just need to talk it over with them, don't you think?"

"Yeah, but…"

"But what?"

"Wouldn't it be kind of a cool surprise for Pops? If he got his Christmas wish after all?"

"Is that what you're asking? If we can pull off this wedding in time, only without your dad knowing?"

"Never mind. It's too much. I shouldn't—"

Penny laughed from deep in her chest, a laugh of pure delight. "I think it's an awesome idea. And hey, a family tradition, surprise weddings, right?"

Ben grinned.

"But surprising your mom is a whole different level of issues."

"I was going to talk to her because I know wedding junk is important to women. I just didn't want to say anything if pulling this off was asking too much of everyone."

"It's a lot," Penny admitted. "I won't lie to you."

"Then never mind. I know I screwed all this up. I should have—"

She placed a hand on his arm. "I'm not saying it can't be done." A smile spread. "This town adores your mom, and everyone is really happy Jackson's back. He's doing so much for everyone. We will get this done." How, she wasn't sure, but regardless, she was already making lists in her head.

"Really?"

"Really. You and I, young Jedi, are going to make this thing happen." She stuck out a palm.

He high-fived it. "You're the best, Aunt Penny."

"I really am," she said.

Over the next several days, Sweetgrass hummed with activity.

Construction proceeded on the two buildings on the square that Jackson had chosen for his Texas headquarters. He'd decided not to try to hold his company Christmas event in Sweetgrass this first year and chosen instead to bring a select few employees to town for the community Christmas. Thus he didn't need as much housing in a hurry, but he wanted to have some enticing workspace for them to view when they got to town.

For their lodging, he'd asked locals to consider taking in a person or two, so that the employees—all of whom had no family with whom to celebrate—would experience the holiday in a more personal way. Volunteers had been plentiful.

The tree inside the courthouse was the Secret Santa tree, with names attached for those who faced an uncertain holiday. Day by day, those tags disappeared, ornaments springing up in their places. Tree trimming for the tall juniper on the courthouse lawn was a continuing event, as residents dropped by to hang new ornaments to accompany the lights that had been strung at the end of Cookie Day, accompanied by the singing of Christmas carols. Patrons at Ruby's Diner had front row seats to the decorating process, and each day was a feast of discussions on which ornaments were most appealing and which had been contributed by whom. Diners caught one another up on the latest ornament count and composition.

Over in the construction zone, work continued on the new headquarters of Enigma Games and the studios on the floor above.

"You ever get tired of pulling a fast one on your buddies?" Ian asked as he measured window trim.

"Hell, no," Mackey snickered. "Why would I?"

"Don't be smug just because you're already married. Springing this surprise on Jackson after doing the same to me...you ready to be zinged right back when you least expect it?"

Mackey's grin was unrepentant. "You trying to tell me you're not crazy happy with Scarlett?"

"Hell, no."

"Do you mind that the surprise meant you had to get married again by the justice of the peace because you didn't have a marriage license?"

Ian rolled his eyes. "Texas law says she had to be there to get one." His smile spread. "But by then, she was committed."

"Then I rest my case. Wiz will love this, you know. It's one crazy great surprise. Ben's such a good kid."

"He is." Ian glanced around them. The construction crews Jackson had hired worked all day, but the locals pitched in where they could, and many of them gave up their evenings to help out. The downstairs of the old dry goods store was taking shape, and up here, living quarters were emerging from what had been abandoned storage for longer than Ian had been alive. "It's a good thing we're doing."

"Yep." Mackey hammered in another nail. "I was

thinking…Roundtree might want in on this."

"The construction? Seriously?"

Mackey shook his head. "He's out on tour. I meant the wedding. The community Christmas celebration. He doesn't really have any family to speak of. He seemed to get a real kick out of being here and singing at your wedding."

Ian smiled. "It was pretty amazing. Not a lot of folks can say they had a country superstar serenade at their wedding. Should we ask Josh to check with him?"

"Quinn's over there working. Let's see what he thinks. Roundtree and Josh have been friends a long time."

Ian glanced over at the silent, watchful presence. Quinn Marshall had been through tragedy, had nearly died. But he'd come out the other side, marrying the former Lorie Chandler, queen of the daytime soaps, a beautiful blonde who'd been stalked by a sicko who'd murdered her first husband. Now they lived on Quinn's ranch up on the Caprock where he raised horses, and she was a midwife, of all things.

Life had interesting twists. Who could have predicted his own? "Yeah, let's see." As they walked over, Mackey asked, "Did you hear that Dev Marlowe might bring his brother Connor?"

"Former SEAL? Got hurt bad in Afghanistan?"

"Yep. Dev says he'd like Connor to get involved with Rissa's therapy horses."

"The vets she's worked with from the Army hospital in San Antonio have really benefitted." Ian knew it was a cause dear to not only Mackey's heart but Bridger's.

Speaking of the devil…

"Bridger, did I hear that your sister is coming for Christmas?"

The man's face lit. "She is. Just found out yesterday." Bridger had lost his entire family when his father had murdered his mother, then killed himself, and Bridger had been considered too young to be allowed custody of his siblings. Dev had helped him find Molly, but two siblings were still missing.

"That is fantastic. Congratulations." Ian extended a fist-bump, and Bridger returned it.

"Yeah. I'm pretty happy. She'll be here the day before Christmas Eve. She's a resident, so time off isn't exactly easy to get, but somehow she managed."

"Nice Christmas gift."

"It is. I'll be able to show her where Penny and I are building our home."

"You're pouring the foundation this week?"

"That's the plan."

"Need any help?"

"Only with getting Legs to say yes." His eyes darkened but his kept his smile in place.

"We could always include her in the surprise wedding," Mackey offered. "Wouldn't be the first time for a double wedding the brides didn't expect."

Bridger didn't echo Mackey's grin. He shook his head. "No. She'll get to it when she does. I'm not pushing her on this." But his sorrow was evident.

Ian clapped him on the shoulder. "Gallagher women…what can I tell you?"

"Anybody have a clue what the problem is?"

"Besides rock-hard heads, you mean?" Mackey asked. "Pure-dee meanness is my explanation."

"Penelope isn't mean. Neither is Rissa or Scarlett, for that matter."

"And yet...they resist."

The three shook their heads in commiseration.

"Well, we're headed to talk to Quinn. Good luck, man. Too bad you can't find yourself a kid who needs adopting to give Penny some urgency."

Bridger chuckled. "Yeah, right. Great tip. I'll keep my eyes peeled."

Then there were the wedding preparations, conducted in secret, mostly at Jeanette's little house.

"I never thought I'd be grateful to see Jackson leave town," Veronica said as she helped Jeanette pin a bodice to a skirt for Beth's dress.

"Keeping secrets is hard."

"Especially when it's something I know he still wants, however much he's let the subject go. And, of course, I can't say a word in front of the twins. Beth would have trouble keeping the secret, but Abby...?"

The group chuckled. "She'd probably pop from the pressure of an unvoiced thought." Rissa grinned. "Love that kid."

"Me, too. But I'm about to pop myself. And I'm nervous."

"Seriously?" Penny asked. "Why? The man adores

you to distraction."

"I know. But so much could go wrong."

"You'll be there, Jackson will be there," Jeanette ticked off on her fingers. "Everyone who loves you will be there. And no one's going to give a rat's patootie if some little detail goes awry."

"You're right. I know you're right."

Even Hayley was hanging around and pitching in. "If I had a man who loved me the way that man loves you..." She looked around. "All of you. It's sickening and gives me hope, all at the same time." Her voice wobbled, and the whole room went still in shock. *Hayley? Emotional?*

She glanced up from the needle she'd proven surprisingly adept at wielding. "Oh, grow up. You know what you have here. Sweetgrass is the perfect town."

Eyebrows lifted. Glances were exchanged.

"Are you okay, Hayley?" Penny probed.

"What? Of course I am. It's no one's fault that some men are blind and stupid besides." She shuddered dramatically. "Anyway, I belong in L.A.—not that visits here aren't nice, but—"

"Nordstrom is in Austin. We'll indulge in some emergency shoe therapy. You'll feel much better," Penny said.

Rissa snorted in derision. "Getting lightheaded from lack of shopping, Hayley?"

Her sister glared at her.

Rissa rolled her eyes.

Veronica cleared her throat and drew attention away from the potential argument. In the week and a half since Ben had dropped his bombshell and planning had whipped into warp speed, they'd become a cohesive group, even sharing confidences. "Steph will be coming with Jackson's group."

"Who's Steph?" Hayley asked.

"One of the three who helped Jackson start Enigma. She's the one Ty tried to frame, then abducted and held hostage before he shot himself right in front of her."

"Oh. Wow. She and Jackson are close?"

Closer than anyone here knew, but Veronica tried to lock that out of her brain. The thought that this woman had seen Jackson naked caused her more than a little lost sleep, no matter how he insisted—and she believed him—that it had been only one time. That it had been only sex.

Only sex was not a term she could relate to. Making love with Jackson was an extraordinary and emotional experience, a time when they fortified their bond, when they left behind business plans and children's needs and decisions that impacted others. In those sacred moments, the world was only the two of them, a private space that felt…hallowed. She restored her soul there. She opened her heart fully. It was every bit as emotional as physical.

She wanted to tear Steph's hair out by the roots.

She felt truly sorry for what Steph had been though.

She didn't want to welcome Jackson's former lover into her home.

But she would. For Jackson.

"So, wait…she's coming here? I thought she wasn't working for him anymore."

"She's not," Penny spoke up. "But that's who my

brother is. He feels responsible for her, for all of them. He's not just their boss, he's their mentor, their cheerleader, their trailblazer. If you could see how people look at him back there...they'd walk through gunfire for him. He has the lowest turnover rate in the industry and yes, he provides terrific benefits to them, but that's not what makes them stay. It's respect. Admiration. And they honestly like him. He's as likely to play a pickup basketball game as lead a meeting. He doesn't put on airs. He has a fancy office for when he needs it to impress outsiders, but he has a workspace like the rest of them, down on the same floor, right in the mix. It's why he wants as many of them here as possible, so that chemistry will survive. If he's gone for months at a time, even conference calls won't make up for not having him there to tell a joke to or to jump in on a *Lone Assassin* tournament." She shook her head. "Until I started working with him, I didn't realize just how hard it was going to be on him to move to Sweetgrass."

"I should have moved to Seattle with the kids," Veronica said.

"No. That's not what he wants at all. He sees how you thrive here. He gets Sweetgrass as only someone who's been estranged from it for so long could. He's just trying to find his footing. He's been solitary for a long time," Scarlett reminded her. "He loves it here, too."

"I admire what you're doing, Veronica. I don't know if I could welcome Steph here, but you're showing Jackson how much you love him by making the effort. I hope you know he only thinks of her as a friend." Penny's expression made it clear that she, too, was aware that the two had had more than a business relationship.

"I believe that." Mostly. It wasn't Jackson she doubted. But how could any woman experience the power and beauty of his lovemaking and not be at least half in love with him? She forced herself to stop and think. Who had Jackson asked to marry, after all?

But Stephanie Hargrove was a bombshell, for sure. Veronica might be a farm wife, but she didn't want to look like one. Not when a breathtakingly handsome man like Jackson was looking at her.

"Having her here will be fine," she said firmly, then switched the subject. "Is Bridger excited about Molly being with him for Christmas?"

Penny cocked one eyebrow at the switch but played along. "He's over the moon. Molly's great."

"All right," Jeanette spoke up. "Time for the attendants to model their gowns."

Rissa groaned. "Girl clothes."

But Penny beamed. "Our dresses match my eyes. Perfect."

"They were intended to match Jackson's," Jeanette reminded her.

"Lucky we're twins, huh?"

"Uncle Tank?" Ben said, crossing the second floor of the old dry goods store.

Tank Patton glanced up from where he was working on installing a door. "Did you need something?"

Ben swallowed. He'd been afraid of his mom's brother for a long time. Folks in Sweetgrass considered him a bully, and the kids at Ben's school either feared him or talked bad about him. At best, he'd been a thorn in Ben's side, and they'd had little to do with him while Ben was growing up.

But recently his mom had explained about the abuse his uncle had shielded her from when they were growing up. Their father Vernon Patton had been a cruel man, and though Ben couldn't say he understood Uncle Tank, really, or even liked him much…maybe he could picture a little how he'd feel if anyone ever raised a hand to Abby or Beth.

He'd kill them, for sure. The idea of violence was foreign to him, since he'd been raised with love surrounding him all his life, but he'd fight to defend his family in a heartbeat.

His mom and Uncle Tank hadn't been so lucky, he'd learned. Ben thought maybe he could see how living in a state of war could change everything.

Lately, his mom had been encouraging Uncle Tank to come around, including him in family meals and such. His uncle was a deputy sheriff whose territory included the whole county, and his schedule was unpredictable so he wasn't around often, but…maybe he wasn't so bad after all.

Ben screwed up his courage. "I was wondering if I could talk to you about the wedding."

Tank's brows snapped together. "I thought you were okay with it."

"I am," Ben hastened to reassure his uncle. "Really, I am." He hesitated. "You don't really like my dad, do you?"

Uncle Tank's mouth twisted. "I'm trying to." After a pause he continued. "Veronica loves him, and he's turning out to be good for her, but—" His gaze whipped to Ben's. "He wasn't always."

Ben still didn't really know everything that had happened between his parents, but he tried to imagine how he'd feel if he'd lost his mom and his father had hated him, the way his pop's life had gone. He screwed up his courage again. "I'm positive he didn't want to hurt her."

Tank grunted. "He got her pregnant and left town."

"But he didn't know, Uncle Tank. He would have stayed if he'd known about me."

His uncle shook his head as if he wasn't convinced. "No point in arguing over that. Point is, your mama loves him and you love him, and we'll get along. Somehow," he muttered.

"Is it only Mom that's the problem you have with him?"

Uncle Tank looked away. "Bad blood goes a lot farther back, but it's water under the bridge now."

"I could…listen. If you wanted to talk."

His uncle eyed him curiously. "I think you mean that."

"I do."

Tank turned back to his work. "Old news," he said. "Grab the other side, would you?"

Ben hastened to help. They worked in silence for a few minutes.

"So what was it you wanted to ask me?"

"Well, see, since my father doesn't know about this wedding, I just—he needs to know I'm good with this because he left it up to me, see. But the girls and Mom want him to be surprised and—"

"What about you?"

"What?"

"Do you want him to be surprised?" Tank asked. "My old man didn't like surprises. Things went bad when he was taken unawares."

Wow. Ben didn't know how to answer that, and Uncle Tank looked uncomfortable now.

He had to say something and make it right. "Um, well…he told Mom the only Christmas present he wanted was for her to marry him, and then when I wasn't sure what to do about him wanting to adopt me—"

"You're his. Why would he need to adopt you?"

"I don't know exactly. My dad—um, David is on my birth certificate, so I guess that has to be corrected."

"And Jackson just left it up to you? He was willing to wait for you?" Uncle Tank looked at him like he must be hearing things.

"He did."

Tank's eyebrows rose, but he said nothing.

"Um…so I can't keep the surprise if I tell him now, but he needs to know I'm okay with it at the wedding."

His uncle was frowning, but he didn't interrupt.

"So I was wondering…I know Mom has asked you to give her away, but I was wondering if I could maybe help with that."

"How?"

Ben shrugged. "Maybe walk on her other side or something? So Pops would know I'm okay with it?" He felt his face heat. "That sounds stupid, right? I just…he's made it clear that I have to agree to be adopted, and now

Mom's all excited about the surprise, but I just can't figure how…"

"I think that would be fine."

"I just can't see—" Ben broke off. "Really?"

Tank nodded. "Really. But you're the one with all the words, so you have to figure out what we say."

Ben swallowed hard. "For real, Uncle Tank?"

"Yeah."

"Thank you. I'll figure out something great to say, I swear it." Then he grabbed his big, formidable uncle in a hug that seemed to shock his uncle as much as it did Ben.

His uncle immediately stiffened, but just as Ben was about to draw away in embarrassment—

His uncle kind of hugged him back. Just for a second.

Ben realized he wasn't sure anyone had ever hugged his uncle before.

"Thanks, Uncle Tank. You're awesome."

His uncle's eyes flew wide. Maybe he'd been thought of as a bully so long that no one had ever seen that he could be anything else…

Ben would have to think about that.

Then his uncle turned away quickly. Cleared his throat.

Ben didn't know how to handle any of this, so he, too, stepped away. "Well, um…thanks again, Uncle Tank. I'll—I'll talk to you soon, all right?"

His uncle didn't turn around but only nodded.

Ben walked away.

But couldn't help looking back.

And wondering.

Chapter Eight

Jackson flew back with a plane full—eight of his key employees, none of whom had families and who were willing to travel, even if they weren't sure about the eventual goal of relocation.

He'd just have to show them Sweetgrass and hope for the best. Nearly two weeks had flown by as he'd worked morning, noon and night with hired help and donated help, all with the goal of setting up Sweetgrass to shine its best.

But he might as well be taking them all to the dark side of the moon, for all that it resembled anything this bunch had ever experienced.

This might not work.

But he hoped it would. Wanted that a lot.

However things went, though, he was going home to Vee. To his kids. To his friends and family, for the first Christmas he wouldn't be spending trying to forget what one could be like. Trying to pretend it was just another day. Working most of it.

He felt like a kid at... He smiled. At Christmas.

"Penny for your thoughts," Steph said. "But sit down. My neck hurts, craning so high."

He realized he'd been pacing the plane, so eager he was to get home. If he could shove the plane through the air to cut down the time, he would. He might not get to marry Veronica at Christmas, but he still had Veronica. She was the real gift, her and their children.

They were his children by heart, legal yet or not.

And Christmas was so going to rock. The cargo space was full of toys and clothes and books he'd bought on a shopping spree to bring home for Secret Santa.

Including a Santa suit. He wasn't sure yet who he was going to con into playing Santa, but Harley seemed like a good prospect. The thought made him chuckle.

"What?" Steph asked.

He sat down across from her. "There are such characters in Sweetgrass. I think you're going to have a great time."

"I still don't think it's smart for me to stay with you and your family."

"Why not?"

The new Steph was a shadow of the old *femme fatale*. This one was much more subdued, but in this second, a little of the old Steph popped up. "Seriously? We've been more to each other than just coworkers, J. Veronica may be a saint, as you insist, but no woman is going to like that." She shook her head. "It won't work, and I'm not wrecking your Christmas by trying."

The woman who had once taken nothing seriously had been replaced by one who was sometimes too quiet, others too angry.

But he couldn't abandon her. She'd been a part of building Enigma, and though Ty's breakdown might not be all Jackson's fault, he felt like it was.

He owed her.

He wanted to fix her.

Surely Sweetgrass would help.

"I'm not going to make you stay there, Steph, I just thought it might be good for you. But if you really don't want to, Aunt Ruby would let you stay at her place, I'm sure."

"Can't I just get a hotel room in Austin? Then you can have your family time, and I'll just pop over now and again."

He knew that was what she wanted, to burrow away again. To hide like a wounded animal. Healing was going to take time, and the wounds were fresh still, but…he just couldn't let her fade away. Her plight might not be all his fault—but he bore the brunt of it, for not seeing what was happening with Ty, if nothing else.

He crouched in the aisle beside her seat. "Please give this a try, Steph. I know it's not what you're used to, but these are good people. They just might restore your faith in human nature."

A mirthless laugh. "Doubtful." She turned away and stared out the window. "How much longer?"

Too long, he thought, itching to see his family again.

While worried that his whole crew would hate Sweetgrass if they wouldn't give it a chance.

He stood up. Raised his voice so everyone could hear. "Listen up, people."

The talk slowed, then ceased.

"I can't explain Sweetgrass to you in terms you'd understand. I can't make you feel what I feel when I'm there." He paused. "I also can't promise nirvana there."

"Come on, boss man. Cows and empty space...that's not heaven?" But Vinny Mattucci was grinning. "Just tell me there's a hot cowgirl or two wearing tight jeans."

"Or a little bitty skirt with boots," called out Ted Bickham.

"You guys are disgusting," said his lone female producer, Gillian Simmons.

"You know you're hoping for a cowboy with a big...belt buckle," yelled Damon Griffin, called Big D because he was about five foot six and one-twenty, soaking wet.

He glanced at Steph and saw a faint smile. He'd take a boatload of teasing if doing so would obtain that result.

He looked up again and knew that Sweetgrass was likely no better prepared for his geeks than they were for his town. This might prove a disaster of epic proportions.

"There are definitely hot women in Sweetgrass." He smiled slowly. "But most of them are related to me. So...behave yourselves, all right? Give the town a chance."

Most of them nodded, willing, if clearly skeptical.

It was all he could ask.

"Bridger, this is beautiful," his kid sister Molly said. She gestured with a sweep of her arm. "Look at this view...amazing. Your front porch?"

He nodded and took in again the sight that never ceased to move him. "Two big rockers right here. I'm going to make them myself. Quinn Marshall said he'd help if I needed it. He's made all kinds of furniture for their home."

"I still can't believe you know Josh Marshall's brother."

"Josh, too. He helped us with the courthouse and put in time here last weekend, working on the old dry goods store renovation." He grinned, reading her mind. "And yes, he and the rest of the Marshalls will be here for the Christmas celebration and the wedding that's still, to everyone's astonishment, a surprise for Jackson."

"That's just so fantastic. Would be even if The Sexiest Man Alive weren't in attendance."

"But nice that he will be, right?" There were stars in her eyes, and Bridger smothered a chuckle.

She tried for a shrug, but gave in and squealed. Jumped up and down a couple of times. "No one back in Chicago will believe me—I guess it's too much to ask to take a selfie with him?"

"That's not how we behave around him here. It's why he and Walker Roundtree like to visit, because they're treated as regular people. Which, if you spend any time with them, you'll discover they both actually are. Neither one has a big head."

"Walker Roundtree? For real?" Her eyes were big as saucers. "What is it about this place? Oh. My. Gosh. I want to call my friend Charlene so bad!"

"But you won't," he said sternly.

A sigh. "I am an adult, Bridger."

"If a starstruck one." He grinned.

"I'm only human. Okay, one more squee, then I'll settle down." She squealed really loud, jumped around in a circle for about ten hops, then stopped. Cleared her throat. "All right. I'm in adult mode from here on."

"Why start now?" he teased and hugged her to his side.

They stared out at the view in silence. "This is a good home," she murmured with reverence. "You've never had that, not really."

He shrugged. "Water under the bridge."

She wouldn't be brushed off. She turned to him, all five feet four of her, bright hair bouncing, and gripped his arm. "Don't make light of it, Bridger. This is huge, what you've found here. Family, friends, a woman to love you…and this—" She stared out again, holding onto him. Then she nestled against his bicep, her head inches below his shoulder. "I had a home…after. But you never did."

"It's fine. I'm fine."

Her face tipped up to him. "I know you are. You make the best of things. I was young back then, but you always did, didn't you?"

"Not really. I was mad as hell back then. Angry and frustrated because Mom wouldn't—"

"Wouldn't leave him?" she paused. "I heard you once. You were begging her to go, to take us away. You said you could work and make us money. You were, what, fourteen?"

"Something like that." Thirteen, actually.

"She would never leave him. I couldn't understand

what was happening the way you did, but…our father wasn't always terrible, right?"

Oh, no. A man who'd murder his children's mother, then take the easy way out and off himself, leaving them to face the disaster, that's not so bad, right? He ground his teeth and remained silent.

But she seemed to see more than he might want. "Of course what he did was horrible. I know that, even if you shielded me from most of it."

"Most of it? You wound up with strangers! That's not bad? You saw me go batshit crazy and try to kill two cops!"

"You didn't try to kill them," she said patiently. "Even that young, I understood what was happening. You were trying to get to us, and they wouldn't let you. You wanted to protect us, as always."

"Great job, huh? Kathleen and Nathan still missing, so many years you and I have lost—" He stalked off and wrestled his emotions under control.

She approached him on silent feet. "But we have each other now. You found me. I'm doing well. I'm happy. You're doing great—and you're about to be much better once you marry Penny."

"If I get to marry her," he muttered.

"What's that?" When he wouldn't face her, she stepped around. Looked him square in the eye. "Bridger, you can't think she doesn't love you. I've watched you together. Anyone can see that in five seconds."

"Then what the hell is she waiting on?" he exploded.

She took a step back.

"I'm sorry."

"It's okay."

"It's not—" He ground his jaw. "It will be all right. It will. She just needs time." Though what the hell for, when he'd given her every reassurance he could come up with, he had no idea.

He exhaled in a gust. Turned back. "We'll end up fine. She's just...scared."

"Of what?"

"She doesn't think she's any good at love."

"She's full of love, from what I can tell." Molly's face split in a grin. "Which is not to be confused with being a soft touch. She does protect her shell, doesn't she?"

"She left D.C. for me. It wasn't her idea to live in Sweetgrass, it was mine. There is a ton of baggage from her past, and being here still hurts her a little, I think...but she came. For me." A quick, rueful grin. "It's like hunting."

"Hunting? And she's what, a deer?"

Bridger chuckled. "I'll call you a liar if you repeat that."

Molly giggled. "Yeah, I don't want to see you dismembered. Death by stiletto and sharp tongue."

"That's my Penelope."

"Anyone can see that she's crazy about you."

"I know. She's survived for years by not letting herself feel. An asset when you're a shark lawyer, but when you're the object of a man's affection...not so great." His mouth quirked. "But you can't say you love someone then spend all your time trying to change them. Rissa says some horses have to be led to believe it's their idea."

"First hunting, now training a horse. Do yourself a

favor, big brother. Refrain from saying these things out loud in her presence."

"What? Do I look stupid?" He shook his head. "Stupid in love, yeah...but I don't have a death wish. I may know a dozen ways to kill someone, but Penelope? She can dismember without leaving a scratch."

"You are gooey over her, aren't you?"

Bridger stared out at the view. If she wasn't ready to marry by the time he had the house done, he'd push and push hard. But he was the one who'd set that self-imposed deadline and was determined to stick to it. She had to be sure...and he needed her to be.

Because once she was his, that was it for both of them. He'd never love another the way he loved her.

"Maddie, prop your feet up on the dash," Boone urged the next day. "Your ankles are swelling." He grunted. "Much as I love my family, you should not be traveling right now. Sitting in the car for hours is bad for you."

"I'm fine, Boone, I swear. And I wouldn't miss this for the world." She glanced over and sighed, reluctantly complying. "There." She propped first one foot, then the other on the dash.

Boone waggled his eyebrows. "Still some mighty fine legs you got there, babe."

She snickered. "How would I know? This is the only time I've seen them in weeks."

"This pregnancy has been harder on you than the

others." He took one hand from the steering wheel and covered hers. "I'm sorry. We'd better make this one the last."

She stroked his jaw. "I'm not ready to say that. I love having your babies, Boone."

"Beats me why you would." He jerked his head toward the seat behind them where Dalton and Sam were quibbling over whether Iron Man or Wolverine was tougher.

"Daddy!" squealed their youngest, her face littered with cracker crumbs. "Love you, Daddy," Lilah Rose cooed.

Boone caught his baby girl's gaze in the mirror. "Love you too, sweetie."

She shifted her gaze to her mother. "Love you, Mama."

Maddie contorted on the seat to cover Lilah Rose's little foot. "Hey, baby girl. You doing all right? Ready to see Aunt Ruby and Ian and Scarlett?"

"And Bwidge! My Bwidge! Love Bwidge."

"That damn Bridger stole my best girl," Boone muttered, then winked.

"I thought I was your best girl," Maddie replied.

"You—" He reached for her, cupped her cheek. "—Are my woman. Whole different deal." He kissed her with his eyes, stroked one long finger over her lips.

Maddie sighed. "I thought we were supposed to be bored with each other by now."

Boone snorted. "Not happening, Granola Girl. Don't know how it could, seeing's how you're the sexiest, craziest woman I ever met. Never a dull moment."

Maddie smiled and sighed, then arched her back and groaned softly.

"Maddie, this is crazy. We should be home in Morning Star. You cannot be standing on your feet for hours, helping out with this monster celebration. That's why we brought in help at the Dinner Bell. And it's Christmas."

"Scarlett's pregnant, too. And it's family Christmas. I love your family. I adore getting all of us together."

"I don't give a good damn," he growled out. "They may be my family, but you're…you. I will not have you endangering yourself."

She giggled.

His head whipped toward her. "This is not funny."

"It kinda is." She caressed his thigh. "Boone, it's just part of being pregnant. I'm not sick, nothing's wrong…I just needed to stretch my back."

"I want to take you back home and put you to bed. Wait on you hand and foot if it'll keep you resting."

She rolled her eyes at him. "I love how you become such a bear, all growly and protective, when I'm carrying your babies." She smiled softly and stroked his cheek. "I'm really okay. Let's just stop for minute and walk around. Then it's only another hour to Sweetgrass."

He began looking for a place to pull over. "Thank goodness Scarlett has backed off on her plans for Ruby's Dream. It's an impossible task, trying to run both restaurants with only the folks in Sweetgrass. She can't possibly maintain what she's attempting to build."

"She's trying to help her Nana save the town, she and Ian."

"Jackson's company moving to Sweetgrass will do more than the courthouse events center ever could. She needs more experienced help than she has there. She needs someone like you—" His gaze whipped to hers. "But not you. You can't keep running down here every time something's going on. Not even for yet another surprise wedding." He shook his head. "Of course you would be in the thick of the planning."

Her smile was unrepentant. "The other one worked out great, don't you think?"

Boone rolled his eyes. "I know it's been killing you to only help out long distance."

She rubbed her hands together. "Jackson is going to be one very happy man tomorrow night."

Boone already knew he was spitting in the wind, trying to argue his wife out of wading into family, neck-deep. Maddie had had too little family in her life until she'd come to Morning Star after his father had bequeathed her Boone's ranch—without Boone's knowledge. She'd arrived from New York full of attitude and sass, intending to leave as soon as the mandated thirty days was up, and here she was, seven years and four children later.

"You are so beautiful."

"What?"

"You changed my life, you know that? Crazy-ass city girl, climbing through weeds and barbed wire in sandals and sundress. I thought you were insane."

She smiled.

"But I couldn't take my eyes off you."

"I aggravated the living daylights out of you at first."

"That you did. But I wanted you more than I'd ever wanted anything in my whole existence."

She stroked her burgeoning belly. "I'd say you got me good."

He laid his hand on hers, then stroked the mound where their unborn baby slept.

And got a kick of thanks.

He couldn't help grinning. "This one is active enough for two."

"You're telling me. I shouldn't be this big. I think this little one just needs more room for the gymnastics."

"Lilah Rose was more active than even her big brothers." His eyebrows rose.

Maddie grinned. "Think you're up for another baby girl, Daddy?"

"Dear, sweet heaven." He shook his head. Then laughed. "Yep. Even another Lilah Rose. Saints preserve us." He adored his little girl, but she was a handful. Two rambunctious boys couldn't hold a candle to how Lilah Rose had swept through all their lives. A Queen Bee in the making.

Maddie laughed softly. "I hear that."

He squeezed her hand and she squeezed right back.

"I got an interesting call while you were packing the truck," she said. "I forgot to tell you."

"From who?"

"Spike."

"New York Spike? Temperamental pastry chef Spike?"

Maddie nodded. "One and the same."

"What did she want?" He'd never met the woman,

but he'd heard a lot about her.

"She's hitting the road again."

"Again? Have mixer will travel? You met her at Sancerre, right?" The five-star restaurant Maddie gave up to live in Morning Star and buy a diner instead.

"Yep." Maddie grinned. "I told her to head for Sweetgrass."

Boone's eyes popped. Then he burst out laughing. "I thought you loved Scarlett."

Maddie laughed, too. Boone pulled the truck into a little rest stop and killed the engine.

"Good night nurse, Miss Maddie. What have you done?"

She winked. "Gotten your cousin the best pastry chef on two continents."

"They'll kill each other." Boone shook his head. "Spike. In Sweetgrass." He laughed helplessly. "Like I said, crazy as a bedbug…but damn sure never boring."

Maddie grinned as he rounded the truck and helped her from her seat. He tapped her nose, then pressed a quick kiss to her lips. "Well, this is gonna be interesting…"

Then kids started piling out of the truck, and Daddy's little girl was lifting her arms to be next.

Never a dull moment.

Chapter Nine

Veronica stirred, feeling strong arms around her, a big, warm body spooning hers.

"Merry Christmas," rumbled Jackson's voice.

His hands began to wander.

Veronica smiled. Twisted to look over her shoulder at him. "Merry Christmas."

The electric blue eyes flared. "This is the best Christmas of my life."

Guilt, mingled with anticipation, had her pressing her lips together. A thrill ran through her for the surprise she desperately wanted to manage to pull off tonight. "It's barely started."

His arms wrapped her midriff and gently squeezed. "The best gift I ever imagined is right here." He laid a hot kiss to her throat.

She shivered. And purred. Rolled toward him.

"Mommy?" came the stage whisper from outside their door. "Prince Daddy? I think maybe Santa came."

Veronica grinned and shook her head. "Welcome to Christmas with kids."

His entire face lit, and he chuckled. "Sleep is overrated." Then he placed a kiss to her throat, over her collarbone…

"Mommy?"

Jackson let his head fall back with a sigh. "I adore those girls."

Veronica took his face in her hands and pressed one soft kiss on his mouth. "But knockout drops have their appeal, yes?"

He grinned, then vaulted from the bed, pulled on jeans and grabbed a shirt. Looked back at her with a wink. "We'll continue this later. It's a date?"

Oh, if only you knew… They had a date with Judge Porter, then Rissa and Mackey were taking the kids for the night. Boone and Maddie and their brood were staying at the Star Bar G, and it would be a madhouse.

But she and Jackson would be alone. For the first time.

She stretched and smiled, watching his hot gaze scan her.

"So not fair, Vee."

"Prince Daddy, are you awake?"

Jackson blew Veronica a kiss and waited for her to slip on the gown he'd stripped off her first thing last night once they'd finally gotten the girls to sleep. He opened the door. "Hey, Princess. Merry Christmas!"

Abby squealed. "Merry Christmas, Prince Daddy!" Veronica spotted Beth wriggling behind her while Abby bounced like a jumping jack.

Veronica heard Ben's door open.

"Merry Christmas, son," Jackson said.

Ben grunted and mumbled a response. He was not a morning person.

"Mommy, Mommy!" The girls raced past Jackson and threw themselves on her bed. "Merry Christmas, Mommy—Santa came!"

Veronica lifted her eyebrows. "I thought the rule was we don't go downstairs to peek until everyone's awake and ready."

Abby grimaced. "Well, um…we were just worried because it's Prince Daddy's first Christmas and what if Santa forgot him and so we—"

"Abigail…?"

Beth covered a giggle.

"Beebee, don't laugh at me."

Beth's brown eyes glittered with suppressed laughter.

Jackson returned with one arm slung around Ben's shoulders.

"Hey, Mom. Merry Christmas." In Ben's eyes she could see their secret bursting to get out.

She understood completely. She wasn't sure how she'd survive until tonight. "Merry Christmas, sweetheart."

"So…what did Santa bring me, Miss Beth?" Jackson asked.

"I didn't—" Beth giggled.

Abby quivered with her own laughter.

"Let's wait for your mom to get ready. Come on out here in the hall. Then we'll all go down together."

The girls scrambled from the bed and raced to catch up. Jackson closed the door, but not before he gave her an exaggerated eyebrow waggle that reminded her of delights in store for later.

If only he knew… He was such a good man. Another man would be sulking over not getting the one gift he'd asked for. Jackson took it in stride and moved on.

A secret shiver rippled through her. He looked so happy.

Just wait until tonight, my love. Every fear she'd had about the wisdom of this surprise evaporated into mist.

He might or might not like the sweater she'd knitted in every stolen moment she could find. It matched his stunning eyes, this present he'd be unwrapping soon.

But he was going to love his real gift when he received it.

"Jackson," she said later, stunned beyond words. Around them were piles of wrappings. He seemed to have bought out the entire West Coast in his quest to shower the children with presents.

They would be having a talk later about what constituted excess.

But right now, she held magic in her hands.

"Do you like it, Vee?" Had she ever heard him so anxious before? "It's not intended to be pushy. I just wanted you to have an engagement ring. The rest will come…whenever. No rush."

She glanced up, and Ben met her gaze, his eyes asking if she would reveal their surprise now.

She gave a faint shake of her head. She would keep Ben's secret until it was time—however hard this ring made keeping her promise. "It's the most beautiful thing

I've ever seen." She gazed up at Jackson with years of love in her heart. "Will you put it on me?"

"Nothing I'd like more. Let me do the honors first...even though there's no candles or moonlight or a fancy dinner."

Even Abby fell silent, as though she understood the import of the moment.

"I thought I would never have the chance to do this." Jackson rose, then went to one knee. "Veronica Patton Butler, love of my life, would you do me the honor of marrying me one day?" His eyes were so blue and so beautiful, so beloved.

He might want candles and moonlight, but this was their life now, the dog chewing happily on a new bone, the children around them, the mounds of crumpled gift wrap...

It was perfect. She cradled his beloved face in her hands. "I've loved you so long, Jackson. Of course I will marry you. There's nothing I want more."

Solemnly he slid the stunning ring over her knuckle. An astonishing creation, the ring seemed nearly gossamer, spun from starlight and dreams, as delicate as a spiderweb and woven in a pattern that, with the wedding ring, formed an intricate pattern.

"The symbol means forever," he said, and raised her hand to his mouth for a kiss.

She lifted her eyes to his. "Forever. I want that."

She had to look at it again. Couldn't get enough. "It fits perfectly." She brushed trembling fingers over it. "I love that you made it so I wouldn't catch it on things as I work." She glanced up again, tears hazing her vision.

"It's stunning. I've never seen anything like it."

"I had it made special for you." He nodded down. "The colored stones on the interlocking wedding band are the kids' birthstones and ours."

Her lips parted. "Oh, Jackson…"

"Because it's all of us. We're together, and we're never going to be apart again." He paused. "And if you wanted to have more, the diamonds can be replaced."

She gazed into his beautiful eyes. "Jackson…"

"It's okay. You've been a mother for a long time. You might not want to do it again, and I'm okay with that. The children we have are plenty."

"Can we think about that?" Though the notion of bearing his child, one they'd raise together from the beginning…

"Of course we can." But longing flickered deep in those electric blue eyes.

She stroked his beloved face and wanted to promise him everything, but she was terrified of spilling the surprise.

Telling him about tonight was tempting, but Jackson deserved to be claimed in front of the whole town. He'd been a pariah once, and he'd suffered alone for years.

They would marry him, all of them, and they'd make him a home.

"I love you so much," she said and went into his arms.

Jackson held her close and kissed her.

Then opened his arms and gathered in the family they would make official tonight.

Penny awoke to the soft warmth of lips tracing a tattoo over her skin.

She gasped as Bridger touched a particularly sensitive spot. "Good morning," she said, eyes still closed.

"Merry Christmas, Penelope." She heard the smile in his voice as he kissed his way down her body.

Then back up, halting at spots that made her sigh. And moan.

And gasp.

She couldn't stand any more, and she grabbed for him. "Come here. Now, now, now," she demanded.

He lunged over her, his big, muscular body a feast, a delight. She let her hands cruise over him, her lips brushing every part of him she could reach, but he stayed maddeningly in control and wouldn't be rushed—

Until he thrust inside her, and her eyes flew open on a gasp.

She smiled. "Merry Christmas to me," she sang, in the tune of Happy Birthday.

Bridger laughed and continued to love her, sweetly at first, then with fire and fury.

She took everything he offered, greedily devoured as much of him as he would allow. Wrapped herself around him like a vine, wanting to stay right here forever, to make love with this magnificent man until neither of them could walk.

Then he fastened his mouth on a spot that made her scream and sent her soaring.

He leaped into the fire after her with a husky chuckle, then a deep, drawn-out, heartfelt groan.

And as they lay there breathing hard, she wondered what on earth she was waiting for. She'd marry him this second.

But tonight was Jackson's night. She couldn't horn in on a dream her brother had cherished for more than half his life.

But soon, she promised Bridger silently. Soon. She wrapped her arms tightly around him. "Best Christmas present ever."

He levered himself up. "I can do better." He stretched across the bed and grabbed something from the nightstand. Returned to her, an uncertain smile on his features.

"What?"

Then she saw the box in his big hands.

The small box.

Her eyes flew wide. "Bridger?"

"Now don't get all worked up, Legs. I'm not making you set any date, all right? I just—" He looked away, then back. "I just want my ring on your finger. I want people to know." He popped open the lid of the box.

She gasped. "That's—"

"Your mother's ring." He nodded. "Your dad offered it to me. I wanted to get you something all your own, but he and Rissa and Jackson thought—"

When she didn't speak, he hastened on. "But I got two bands made that lock together on either side so this is in the middle, see, and they make it all one. Something old and something new and—" His voice faltered. "You don't like it."

"I—" She had to place a hand over her mouth. Tears spilled. "I love it." Her gaze flew to his. "You don't mind that it's Mama's?"

"You don't want to pick out your own? You're not all that traditional, Penelope, and—"

She reared up. Kissed him hard. "Put it on me." Then she glanced at him. "Bridger, we're naked."

A laugh burst from him. "We have to get dressed first?" He shook his head. "You are the damnedest woman. What, you think your mama is looking?"

She couldn't help the squeak that erupted. She grabbed for the sheet. Tried to cover herself, but Bridger was perched over her legs.

He threw back his head and laughed like a loon. "The same woman who seduced me out of my socks from the first moment we met. My Shark Girl who fears no one, who will make out with me anytime, anywhere—" He laughed again. "Give me your hand. You think your mama never got naked with the man she loved?"

Another squeak. "Bridger!"

His grin was wide as the Mississippi.

"Gimme." She leaned closer. "But no one hears this story."

He took her fingers and paused. Leaned into her and laid a slow, sweet kiss on her mouth. "Deal."

"Now."

"So rude. No sense of occasion," he tsked. Then, with his amber eyes smiling as brightly as his mouth, he put the ring over her first knuckle. "Penelope Gallagher, will you marry me at some time and date to be determined by the parties heretofore mentioned in the aforesaid contract of marriage dated—"

"Shut up." She shoved her finger into the ring and grabbed for him.

Caught him off-guard enough to roll him over and straddle the ridged belly that was bouncing with his laughter.

She held out her hand and admired the ring.

"Do you really like it?" he asked, surprisingly vulnerable.

She stopped admiring and caught his gaze with her own. "I love it. Almost as much as I love you." She bent and kissed him slowly, with all the love bursting from her heart. "And I would love to marry you, Bridger Calhoun."

"Merry Christmas to me," he sang.

She buried her face in his neck and breathed him in. "Merry Christmas, my love."

"Bless Texas wintertime temperatures," Maddie said, standing in the open front door of the diner looking at the courthouse lawn several hours later.

"Hear, hear," Rissa agreed, joining her. "They couldn't do that if it was freezing outside."

"What are you two talking a—whoa," Penny chimed in.

"Scarlett, where is—" Lacey Marlowe fell silent. "Wow."

Scarlett spoke. "I'd consider it sexist that we're putting together the meal, except—" She waved her hand toward the pickup football game going on out there.

"Shirts and skins," Sammie Marshall said. "How come they can't both be skins?"

Lorie Marshall chuckled. "We could paint the chests of one team blue instead of them wearing shirts."

It was a remarkable sight, for sure. Josh Marshall, Bridger, Ian, Jackson, Boone and Walker Roundtree were skins. Quinn, Case, Mackey, Dev Marlowe, Tank and Mitch were shirts. The teenage boys were sprinkled among them—Ben playing on his dad's team, Grant Marshall and Davey Gallagher with their fathers on the other.

And they were surrounded by children of all sizes, managing to compete vigorously with one another while watching out for the little ones who wanted to play. Grant's younger sister had drafted Christina Marlowe, Abby and Beth to be cheerleaders.

But Lilah Rose was clinging to Bridger's back like a tick.

"Oh, Bwidge," Perrie sighed and grinned.

"My Bwidge," Scarlett and Rissa echoed.

The women broke up laughing.

"What on earth is keeping you all standing—oh." Melba Sykes stopped in mid-sentence. "Well, now."

Veronica grinned despite her nerves. Jackson looked so happy.

Ian called out his name and aired a long bomb. Jackson loped around behind the rest and caught it for a score.

"We want the ball, Bwidge. Can we get the ball?"

"I don't know what to say," Maddie grinned. "She's all Boone's."

"Uh-huh," Rissa grinned. "Can we make them switch shirts and skins now that one side has scored?"

"I still like the blue paint idea better," Lacey said.

Scarlett sighed. "We'd better get back to work. They'll be starving soon."

"We can take shifts watching," Elena Marshall suggested.

Everyone laughed. They trooped back to uncover dishes and finish putting out paper plates and set up cups beside the vats of sweet tea.

"You ready for this?" Penny asked Veronica.

"Terrified," Veronica responded with a hand on her stomach.

"Ian and Mackey swear they're all set to spirit Jackson away."

"How? He's having the time of his life."

"No idea, but that's not our job. Gorgeous ring, by the way. I got first peek."

"Thank you. It's awesome that you have your mom's. I don't feel quite so bad about laying claim to her dress."

"Don't. We're going to be sharing lots of things from now on."

"Thank you." Veronica's eyes filled.

"For what?"

"For welcoming me. For being a sister. I always wanted one."

"And I always wanted to ditch Ris. Maybe Tank and I can trade."

"I heard that," her sister said darkly.

"Prince Daddy?" Beth looked up at Jackson later as the meal wound down. "Are we going to get married soon?"

He ran a hand over her hair. "I hope so, honey." He looked out over the crowded cafe. Tables and chairs had spilled out onto the green space that ran alongside the diner all the way back to Aunt Ruby's house. He'd thought this event would be held at the courthouse, but Scarlett has said something about repairs being needed in the kitchen, some piece of equipment that would require a warranty call as soon as the holidays were over.

"Have you had a fun day?" he asked Beth.

She leaned into him. "Yes. Even if Mommy thinks you gave us too many presents."

He chuckled. Glanced down. "Is that possible?"

She shrugged. "Some kids don't have any presents ever."

"That's true." But no child in Sweetgrass had gone without presents this year. He'd made certain of that.

Laughter flared in the corner where one of his geeks was holding court, demonstrating a new game he'd come up with and Jackson hoped to license. From the crowd gathered around, the game was a hit.

He glanced over at Steph who was holding an animated conversation with Perrie Gallagher. No idea what that was about, but he was happy to see it.

He saw Ben stop to speak to Jackson's dad, and enjoyed James Gallagher's obvious pride in the grandson he doted on. When Ben and Eric shared a joke with Jackson's dad, he couldn't help but feel like all was right in his world.

He wanted to spirit Veronica away and have the

evening with her by himself, but he couldn't see her. She was probably back in the kitchen. Jackson straightened to go after her, but just then Mackey and Ian approached. "Wiz, we need to talk to you. Can you spare us a sec?"

"Sure. What's up?"

Ian shook his head. "Not here. Let's go to Ruby's house."

Mystified, he glanced down at Beth. "Honey, I'll be right back. You go see your mom, okay?"

"I was going to spirit her away with me," Lorie Marshall said, strolling up. "She and Abby said they wanted my Clarissa to show them something. Come with me, Beth?"

"Okay. Bye, Prince Daddy!" Beth hopped down.

He watched her walk away, then turned to his friends. "What's going on?"

"In a sec," Mackey promised and led the way out the back.

Neither would speak until they got inside the house and went into Ruby's library.

Inside, Ben waited. With a suit in his hands. "We need to get dressed, Dad."

Dad? Jackson's eyes widened. "What for?"

"Because you don't want to marry Mom in those jeans."

Jackson's heart stopped. Literally. "Are you serious?"

His son's eyes glowed. "Completely."

"But—"

Ben handed the suit hanger over to Ian, then turned and grabbed some papers from the desk. "But first, sign these."

Jackson took them. Felt his throat close. "These are—"

"Adoption papers. Aunt Penny drew them up."

A warmth spread through Jackson's chest. "You want this? You're sure?"

"I'd like to keep Butler in my name, if that's okay. Is it? But I want to be a Gallagher legally."

Jackson struggled to find his voice. "It's very okay. David was my friend. He did a hell of a job raising you." Not getting to do so himself would always be bittersweet for Jackson, but he wanted to live for the future, not miss today by mourning the past. "Your mom knows about this?"

Ben's smile widened. "Everyone in town knows but you, Dad. Well, all the adults. No way Abby could keep that secret. It's about killed me."

"It was your boy's idea." James Gallagher's voice came from behind him. "He wanted you to have a Christmas surprise."

Jackson shook his head. "I don't know what to say. This is…perfect, son." He cleared his throat. "You got a pen?"

"Well, actually, you have to do it in front of a notary."

The door opened again. Judge Porter stepped in. "Couldn't help but overhear. I'm legal enough. Go ahead."

"Vee should be here. We should do this as a family."

Ben nodded. "You're right. I just…I wanted to be the one to show you."

Jackson looked again at the document, then back at his son. "You'll never give me a finer gift, Ben." He extended the papers. "Will you keep them safe for me?"

"Yes, sir." Then Ben reached for him, and Jackson embraced the son whose life had changed his world, then and now. He hugged Ben hard, grateful that his boy was holding on just as tightly. Tears stung his eyes. "No one ever had a better son, Ben. I love you."

"I love you, too, Dad. I want to call you Dad. I don't think he'd mind."

The moment was powerful. Painful with the ache of the past and the bright promise of the future. *Let me be enough*, Jackson prayed. *Let me be the father these children need.*

"I'd like that a lot." He swallowed. "So...should I deduce that this is why the dinner wasn't at the courthouse?"

More than one laugh was a little hoarse.

"I can't believe we pulled it off," Ben said. "Keeping the secret was murder."

Jackson mock-frowned. "Don't get too good at deceiving your old man, okay?"

Ben chuckled. "I'm a teenager, Dad. I'm supposed to try to pull things over on you."

Jackson ruffled Ben's hair. Glanced over at his father, who smiled wryly. "A parent's reward. Watching his child have teenagers."

Everyone shared a laugh.

"Well. Guess we'd better get ready, so I can go marry your mom."

"You're gonna swallow your tongue when you see her, Dad."

Jackson smiled. "It's like that every time."

Chapter Ten

The courthouse looked completely different from Scarlett and Ruby's double wedding. Not only the seasonal flowers were different, but the large, glittering tree changed the scene from when Scarlett and Ian, Ruby and Arnie had married here in the fall.

"Brenda, you have outdone yourself," Veronica murmured as she peered over the bannister to the first floor. White lilies she'd grown in a cold frame spilled from baskets lined with evergreen boughs and scarlet pyracantha berries gathered along roadsides and from bushes around Ruby's house.

Brenda had come up with the notion of spraying yucca spears and sumac silver. She'd twined rosemary and wrapped it around the stair rails, adorned with sumac berries sprayed cerulean blue and tied with blue and silver ribbons. Pots of forced amaryllises, both red and striped ones from Veronica's greenhouses, provided lush islands of color.

Her attendants each carried a single amaryllis tied with silver and blue ribbon. Her own bridal bouquet was a mixture of greenery and white lilies tied with silver and blue ribbon the color of Jackson's eyes.

People had begun filtering inside, and Jeanette drew her back to the room she'd used to dress. "You don't want to spoil the surprise."

"I'm so ready to see him," Veronica said. "I wonder how it's going over there."

"It would be great to be a fly on the wall, wouldn't it?" Penny asked, coming up behind them.

Veronica looked up. "You look lovely. And Rissa, look at you!"

Rissa smoothed self-consciously at her cerulean dress. "I like jeans better."

"Yes, but Mackey will choke when he sees you."

"He'd better."

Veronica held out her hands to the two women wearing slim, flowing columns of silk. "I appreciate you standing up with me."

"Where else would we be?" Penny asked.

Then small feet thundered up the steps, and her own twins burst through the door. "Mommy, look! We have beautiful princess dresses—oh!" Even Abby was stunned into silence.

"Mommy, you're so beautiful," Beth said.

"Even prettier than Scarlett," Abby vowed.

"Hey, watch it." Scarlett approached, smiling. "But you're right. Your mother looks like an angel. And anyway, I didn't have the two prettiest flower girls in the universe for my wedding. Why was that, Maddie?"

"Whine, whine, whine. Maybe because it was all I could do to drag you to the altar?" Maddie winced and rubbed at her back.

"You need to sit down. You shouldn't be climbing

those stairs," Lacey scolded.

"Good grief, you're channeling Boone. I'm fine."

The glances exchanged demonstrated that Veronica wasn't the only skeptic. "Maddie, thank you. You did so much from Morning Star. I'm so grateful we get to be family."

Maddie's pinched look dissolved in her typical good humor. "Me, too, cuz." She glanced down at the twins. "And now that we're family, I'm counting on you two to help me ride herd on Lilah Rose."

"We will," Beth pledged solemnly. "Where is she?"

"Downstairs with her daddy. Or Bridger. No telling."

"Oh, Bwidge," several of them crooned.

Laughter filled the space, and Veronica was moved to tears, being a part of them.

"Don't you dare screw up that makeup!" Hayley screeched.

Veronica sniffed. "I wouldn't on a bet." Her stomach was a mass of nerves. "I am so ready."

Just then, a knock on the door. "Mom?"

"Ben." Veronica smiled. "Come in. How is he? How did it go?"

"It was great. Couldn't have been better."

"And he signed."

Ben shook his head. "He said we should do it as a family."

"Aww…" More than one voice sounded.

Ben flushed, then glanced around. "Wow, Aunt Penny, Aunt Rissa. You look so pretty." He looked at Veronica. "Mom, you're beautiful."

She smoothed at the dress that held such history. "I

feel beautiful. And nervous. How much longer?"

"Look at us, Ben! Don't we look like princesses?"

He turned toward his sisters. "You sure do." Then he pivoted back to his mother. "That's why I'm here. Dad's downstairs waiting for you."

"Dad?"

Ben flushed. "He thinks my—Dad David would be okay with it."

"I agree," she said. "I bet Jackson's really happy."

"So…you ready?"

We've waited our whole lives for this moment. "I am. So very ready."

"We'll just head downstairs. Girls?" Maddie held out a hand to each of the twins.

"See you soon, Mommy!"

Veronica bent and hugged them both. "We're going to be so happy together." She watched them skip away, David's girls, and for a moment she had to press her lips together.

Then she and Ben were alone.

"Do you miss him at all, Mom?"

"I do. David was a good man. He loved me well." She studied her tall son's face. "Sure you're okay with this?"

"Yes. And I think he is, too. He always wanted you to be happy. Dad makes you really happy, doesn't he?"

"He does." There were no words for how much.

They heard the music start up, Walker Roundtree and Henry playing guitar as they had for Scarlett's wedding.

A knock at the door. "Veronica?" Her brother's

voice.

"Come in, Tank."

He walked inside, resplendent in a suit.

"Goodness, you look so handsome."

Tank shifted awkwardly. "Thanks." His gaze took her in. "You're beautiful. You always were."

She went to him. Touched his arm, though he wasn't a toucher. "Tank, thank you. For doing this. For welcoming Jackson into our family."

He nodded, his eyes solemn on hers. "You're positive this is what you want? Because I'll take care of you, you know that."

"I do. You've protected me so many times before." She smiled. "But I'll never need protecting from Jackson. He's my heart."

One more solemn nod. "Ben and I thought we'd do this together. You okay with that?"

Tears rushed in again. "That would be wonderful. Thank you both."

So she left the room and descended the stairs with each of them at her side, heading for the man she'd waited so very long to marry. Ahead of her she saw her girls forget their flower petals and start running.

To Jackson.

There he stood, tall and handsome and beloved, his gaze stunned and admiring.

She smiled, and he smiled back.

And it was all she could do not to run to be with him, too.

Jackson thought his heart would stop when he saw her. He knew he should wait, but they'd already waited so long for each other.

He stepped into the aisle as she began her way to him, barely noticed Scarlett take the girls to their seats.

He took another step, and Veronica laughed through her tears.

Then he was in motion, and so was she. As they came together, he swept her up and vowed never to let her go. Eyes closed, feeling her slender arms around his neck, he was overcome with a sense that finally, finally everything fit.

He wasn't sure who was trembling, her or him.

"Dad." Ben approached, and Jackson opened his eyes.

"Dad, you're supposed to let us give her to you," Ben stage-whispered.

The audience laughter spilled in warm waves around them.

But he heard a few sniffles, too.

Her hand stroked down the back of his head. "Jackson…"

He made himself lean back. "Yes?"

A smile filled her eyes, though they glistened with tears. "I love you so much."

He embraced her again, hard. Then, with a deep exhalation, he set her on her feet. "I don't want to let go."

"Then don't. I don't want to, either." She held out

her hand for his. "Walk me the rest of the way?"

"Yes." He didn't care what anyone else thought of his behavior. He'd loved her and missed her for so very long...

They reached Judge Porter, but Jackson halted a step shy. Turned to her. "You're the most beautiful bride in the world. You take my breath away."

"Awww..." More than one voice spoke.

She smoothed his tie. "You do look like a prince, you know."

He could hardly speak, instead brought her hand to his lips.

"So...let's be flexible, shall we?" Judge Porter said over their heads. "Ben, Tank, do you have something to say? Since it appears that the bride you were giving away has escaped you?"

A few chuckles, then a clearing of the throat. Tank. "My sister isn't mine to give away. She's belonged to you for a long time. But you won't hurt her again," he warned.

Jackson turned to face the man who had been a foe when they were younger. He noted the concern, the resolve in Tank's eyes and understood both. "I won't hurt her. I'm sorry I ever did. Thank you for protecting her, growing up. I promise I'll keep her safe from here."

Tank didn't soften the warning in his eyes, but at last he nodded.

Veronica slipped from his grasp and went to her brother. Kissed his cheek. "Thank you. I love you."

More than one sniffle was heard as Veronica turned away, then stopped before Ben and held out her hand.

"Walk me the rest of the way?"

"My pleasure." He closed the short distance and stopped in front of his father. "My sisters and I aren't giving Mom away, we're keeping her—but we're entrusting her to you. She's the best mom in the world, and we believe you'll be a great dad." His young jaw hardened with his own warning.

Jackson nodded his approval. "I will guard her with my life, son, just as I will care for all of you. Thank you for trusting me with the most precious gift in the world."

Judge Porter cleared his throat. "Well, now." He cleared it again. "I was going to say a few words about what it means to unite a family, but seems to me you all have learned that lesson well already. So shall we press on?"

Veronica handed her flowers to Penny, and Ben took his place beside his grandfather, who was serving as best man. Jackson's sisters smiled at him, and Penny blew him a kiss.

Jackson had waited for this day for most of his life.

As Judge Porter readied himself to speak, Jackson made a split-second decision. "May I have a little leeway, Judge?"

"Seems to me that horse is out of the barn," the older man commented.

Laughter rolled through, but Jackson wasn't deterred. He looked behind Veronica. "Girls? Would you come here, please?"

"Beebee, we get to get married!" Abby crowed, and more laughter ensued.

Jackson pivoted to Ben. "Son?"

When they were all gathered, he took Veronica's hands again. "I, James Jackson Gallagher, take you, Veronica Elizabeth Patton Butler, to be my lawful wedded wife, to have and to hold, to honor and to cherish, for richer or for poorer, in sickness and in health, forsaking all others, for as long as we both shall live."

Then he looked at her children. "Elizabeth Anne, Abigail Suzanne and Benjamin Edward Butler, I ask you to be my family from this day forward. I promise to guard you, to guide you to the best of my abilities, to keep you safe until my dying breath."

Beth leaned into his side, and Abby touched his arm. "I love you, Prince Daddy."

"I love you, too—all of you." He looked at Ben.

Ben placed one hand on his back and nodded. "Me, too, Dad."

"Veronica?" Judge Porter smiled at her.

"I, Veronica Elizabeth Patton Butler, take you, James Jackson Gallagher, to be my lawful wedded husband, to have and to hold, to honor and to cherish, for richer or for poorer, in sickness and in health, forsaking all others, for as long as we both shall live." She smiled. "I gladly entrust you with my children, their hearts and their safety. I know you will take care of them—you already have." She squeezed his hands.

He didn't know how his heart could hold any more than it did at this moment.

Judge Porter asked for the rings.

Jackson held the other half of the gossamer ring he'd given her, his hands not quite steady. He looked into her eyes as he spoke, years of loving her echoing through time. "With this ring, I thee wed and pledge my life, my love and my honor, committing my heart and my soul to you and you alone from this day forward." He slid the ring onto her finger, then brought it to his lips.

Abby clapped and jumped. Beth patted his arm.

Ben smiled at him, and Jackson smiled back.

Veronica took his ring and repeated her own vows to him in a voice as clear as angel song. She squeezed his fingers and looked into his eyes. "I love you so much," she whispered. Her eyes shimmered with tears.

His own eyes burned as he looked to each of them in turn and spoke only to them. "Thank you all for the best Christmas of my life."

Penny watched as her brother made his vows to the woman he'd never stopped loving. In a clear, strong voice, he vowed to love and honor and cherish her, to never leave her, and she knew the words held additional meaning for this bride and groom.

Standing up with them, she wished for Bridger beside her. She'd like to take his hand and tell him she was finally ready.

As if he could hear her, he looked up from where he was sitting.

Golden eyes burned. Promised everything she could ever hope for. He would love her with everything in him. He would keep her safe, not only her body, but her heart.

She only hoped she could do justice to his heart, his generous soul. *I love you*, she wanted to mouth. To say out loud.

But this was Jackson and Veronica's time, so she only put her love in her gaze and hoped he could see it. Then she dragged her attention back to the couple pledging their lives right in front of her. She gripped Veronica's bouquet with her own, and she watched her twin slide that astonishing ring on her finger, so much love spilling from his gaze that it swirled in the air around them.

She glanced down at her own ring and knew that though Veronica's was spectacular, hers meant more. *Mama, let me be half the woman you were—no. Help me be every bit as good, as devoted. Bridger deserves all that and more. Please let me be a good mother because, heaven help me, I want to try.*

When Judge Porter pronounced them man and wife, Jackson cradled Veronica's face as if she were all that was precious and right in the world, and he kissed her with love that spilled over all of them.

Penny glanced down at her ring, then over to Bridger. He kept his gaze steadily on her.

"Ladies and gentlemen, may I present Mr. and Mrs. Jackson Gallagher and their family?"

There were cheers. There was laughter. There was applause.

And just when Penny was ready to break away and run to the man she loved, another voice cried out—

"Uh-oh, Boone."

"Maddie?"

"My water just broke."

"Bridger!" Boone shouted.

"Molly—" Bridger called.

Rissa laughed. "Never a dull moment in Sweetgrass!"

Then everything happened at once.

The reception didn't go exactly as planned, but no one seemed to care. Molly and Bridger, in consultation with midwife Lorie Marshall, had quickly determined that Maddie's baby was going to be born in Sweetgrass—and soon, three weeks early or not. Boone had carried Maddie to Ruby's house, where the guest room downstairs had been pressed into service. EMS was headed their way, but they were on the other side of the county.

The contractions were too close together to be driving her to the hospital a hundred miles away, though Jackson had offered his plane or anything they needed. Molly wasn't concerned after hearing the baby's estimated weight at last doctor's appointment and with all vital signs good.

"I'd certainly like better monitoring, I admit," she'd muttered.

"Tell me what you need. You and Bridger make a list. We need a full-service clinic in town, at a minimum," Jackson said. "That goes to the top of my list."

Molly's brows flew, and she and her brother exchanged meaningful glances. "Nice friends you have, bro."

Bridger grinned. "I told you Sweetgrass was unique."

Meanwhile the party had moved to the diner to be closer to Ruby's. Right off, the quilters brought out the wedding ring quilt they'd made for the newlyweds.

Veronica cried and stroked it. "Oh, Melba...Joyce...Earlene...I don't know what to say—oh! Look! That's a piece of Bethie's sundress."

"Ben got into your box of clothes you'd saved from the children." Ruth Sudduth smiled.

"You're not upset, are you?" her sister Linda Vise asked. "We thought you would be pleased to have mementos of your children in it, too."

"I'm not," Veronica assured. She glanced at her son. "Benjamin, I love you."

Ben all but shuffled his feet. "No big, Mom." Then he pointed. "But you may not be real happy when you notice that your holiday apron got cut up." He winced. "I figured that was better than taking any of your clothes. I couldn't find anything from when you were a kid. Are you mad?"

"How could I be?"

Relief swept over his features. "Did you see Dad's jersey Aunt Rissa found from when he was in high school?"

Jackson peered over her shoulder and beamed. "Oh, man...from the year we won State." He clapped Ben on the back, then looked around at the group of women who'd quilted with his mother. "How on earth did you ever get this done?"

"Mel Brown gave up her dining room for us to set up a quilting frame. We've spent so much time together," Linda Johnson joked, "we're sick of each other."

The group laughed. "Not true, Jackson," said Joyce Walden. "We loved your mother. She would have wanted to do this for you herself."

"She would have," he agreed. "We will treasure this." One by one he made his way around, bending from his great height to hug them, Veronica following suit, holding the quilt close and asking for stories of each fabric.

In the far corner of the dining room, Lilah Rose wasn't thrilled that neither of her parents nor her be-loved Bridger were on hand, so Abby and Beth, Davey Gallagher, Clarissa and Grant Marshall plus Christina Marlowe teamed with Perrie to act out one of Perrie's children's stories to the delight of everyone, not just Lilah Rose.

Penny decamped to Ruby's when the other adults assured her they had things well in hand. She couldn't assist Bridger, but she wanted to be close.

He came out to see her once. "It's going fast. No signs of fetal distress, thank goodness, and Maddie's holding up well. She's a natural."

"I heard her chewing out Boone."

He grinned. "Women do that. Scare you off, Shark Girl?"

She screwed up her face. "I like being in control."

He burst out laughing. "No kidding." He bent to her.

"But I make you lose it regularly, don't I?"

She smiled. "That you do."

"And you survive just fine."

She looked at him, stripped down to a t-shirt smeared with unnamed fluids, latex gloves on his hands.

He held fast, no matter what life threw at him. He'd been to war, he'd nearly died. He cradled babies and defended the innocent. He was brave and strong and valiant—

And fun. And, oh yeah, sexy enough to fry her every last nerve ending.

"What? What's going on in that busy brain?"

Let's get married, she thought. *Right now.*

Molly called his name.

"Love you. Gotta go." He kissed her quickly and took off.

She'd never loved him more.

She set off in search of her brother. They'd shared one important date.

Maybe he wouldn't mind adding another.

Jackson laughed when she found him and explained. "Of course I don't mind. I kinda like it." He grinned and looked at the woman he hadn't let go of yet. "Vee?"

"Bridger would be so happy. Of course we don't. But you don't have a wedding dress."

"I don't care. We have to wait and be sure Maddie and the baby are okay first, though."

"Are you worried? Is Bridger?"

"They don't seem to be concerned. Molly says both baby and Maddie are doing well." She chuckled. "Boone's getting the sharp side of Maddie's tongue, though."

Harley Sykes overheard. "It's a man's lot. My Melba cussed me up one hill and down the next."

"What are you saying about me, old man?" Melba called out.

"Nothing—" Harley winked at them and left.

"Leave this to me," Veronica said. "Brenda? Let's go take a look at the flowers."

"No, Veronica—you just got married," Penny protested. "You can't—"

"We'll all help," Jackson said. "Ian, Mackey, let's round up the troops. My sister has decided to uphold the Gallagher wedding tradition."

Just then Bridger burst through the back door. "Lilah Rose?" he called out. "Dalton and Sam? You ready to go meet your new sister?"

"Bwidge!"

The room erupted into relieved laughter.

"Maddie's okay? The baby's okay?"

"They're both fine. The baby is nearly eight pounds, even early." Bridger bent and caught Lilah Rose as she raced pell-mell toward him and her brothers followed. He turned to go.

"Bridger, wait—" Penny called out.

He turned back. "You want to come?"

"No—yes—that's not it."

"Okay…"

She clasped her hands and wrung them. "Bridger, will you marry me?"

He grinned. "Legs, I asked you first. When we were na—" He halted, a devil's gleam in his eyes.

"TMI, my man," Jackson warned. Then laughed. Others joined him.

She tried to ignore them, nerves jumping. "I mean… now."

His brows rose to his hairline. "Now?" He glanced down at his stained t-shirt. "Like *now* now?"

"I'll just take these kids to see their mom," Dev said, scooping up Lilah Rose. "Boys? Lace, come with me?"

"Okay, Uncle Dev," answered Dalton. Sam followed right behind.

"Maddie will want to be there, you know," Lacey murmured to Penny and Bridger as they passed.

"But—" How long would that take?

"Legs, we could wait. It won't hurt anything."

She didn't want to wait now.

"Is that a pout I see, Penelope?" Bridger's grin was irresistible.

Scarlett stepped up. "Maddie's pretty tough. Everyone else is already at the courthouse getting things ready, Bridger. I'll go see what Molly thinks and what Maddie wants to do, okay?" She looked him up and down, then grinned. "Meanwhile, need a new shirt?"

He glanced at himself then back up to Penny with that mischievous grin. "For better or worse, Legs?"

She smiled right back. "I'll take you however I can get you."

He reached for her. "A big hug on that?"

She jumped back. "Eww! Don't mess up my dress!"

"That's my Shark Girl." Bridger threw back his head and laughed.

It was eleven-thirty when Penny finally had her chance, only they weren't getting married at the courthouse, after all. Maddie might be tough, but there was no way Penny was making her travel, even across the town square.

The wedding was to be held in Ruby's parlor. The old house had been built in the late 1800s, and it was an example of old-fashioned grace. The parlor and living room sat across the entry from one another, with sliding doors that could be opened to the foyer and to the formal dining room beyond the parlor.

Half of Sweetgrass was crowded inside, waiting, when Penny made her own trip down Ruby's front staircase on her father's arm.

She was wearing a different gown, one of the only formal ones she'd brought with her to Sweetgrass, never expecting to be married in it.

But it worked for her.

It was siren-red.

She couldn't help grinning as Bridger's eyes just about popped out of his head.

He'd cleaned up nicely, too, in a silver-gray suit borrowed from Jackson and a blinding white shirt with a red tie that fortuitously matched her gown.

Or they had a mole. Veronica, probably. Such a romantic.

Penny was feeling pretty romantic herself right now.

Mackey and Jackson stood up with Bridger, while Rissa and Veronica were her attendants. Veronica still had on her wedding gown, though she'd offered to change.

Penny wouldn't hear of it. She felt like Mama was with them because of the dress. Rissa was still in her cerulean gown from Jackson's wedding. Abby and Beth had had a little nap, and they were reprising their roles as flower girls, too, while Ben played usher.

Maddie was ensconced in a chaise, her sleeping newborn cradled in her arms. Boone stood over them both, their boys at his side and Lilah Rose in his arms. She looked ready to leap toward her Bwidge.

Penny had to smile. Would they have a little pistol like her one day?

Quite possibly. Lilah Rose was a Gallagher girl, after all.

Then she and her father were in front of Judge Porter, who'd also had a nap.

"Who gives this woman?" he asked.

"Her mother and I," James responded. He looked at Penny. "She's here with us. I feel her."

Penny bent her head to her father's shoulder and pressed her lips together. Oh, how she wished she could hug Mama, too. Then she sniffed and straightened. "Thank you, Daddy. I love you." She kissed his cheek.

"Proud of you, Princess." He sent Bridger a mock-glare. "You better take care of her, son. She's precious to me."

Bridger made a solemn nod. "To me, as well, sir. You can count on it."

James smiled. "I believe you." Her father released her to Bridger, and she took his arm.

"Hey there, Legs." He winked. "You sure are gorgeous."

She smiled back. "I wouldn't mind if you suffered a little."

He scanned her in one long, slow roll. "Trust me, I am."

Judge Porter cleared his throat. "An unruly family you have here, James."

"I certainly do, Daniel."

Laughter poured over them like a blessing.

"Well, now. Shall we get on with it?"

Oh, yeah. She was more than ready.

Penny missed half of Judge Porter's words because her gaze was locked on Bridger's, and worlds swirled in those golden eyes. Promises and dreams, delights they would share, so many moments to look forward to…

"Penny?"

"Yes?"

"Would you care to go first, to make your vows to him?"

She smiled into Bridger's eyes. "I really would." And so she began. "I, Penelope Lucinda Gallagher, take you, Bridger McCarthy Calhoun, to be my lawful wedded husband, to have and to hold, to honor and to cherish, for richer or for poorer, in sickness and in health, forsaking all others, for as long as we both shall live."

The old-fashioned words were a comfort, a sealing of a promise that spooled back hundreds of years before the two of them.

She thought about The Lady and her soldier. Where were they now? Had they ever had the chance to make their own vows?

Could they be half so happy?

Bridger began to make his promises in a deep voice, and she was mesmerized by him. Couldn't see anything but this amazing man who had chosen to overlook all that was not easy about her.

"…For as long as we both shall live," he finished.

And didn't smile but instead looked solemnly, seriously into her eyes.

"Do you have a ring for her, Bridger?"

"I do." Then the irrepressible Bridger awoke. He waggled his eyebrows at her, no doubt remembering the morning and their state of undress.

And wanting her to do the same.

Penny had to duck her head and swallow an inelegant snort.

He tilted her chin, his eyes hot and filled with promises. "With this ring I thee wed, and pledge my life, my love and my honor, committing my heart and my soul to you and you alone from this day forward."

"And you, Penelope? Do you have a ring for this man?"

She hadn't until her father had offered his until they could replace it. Thank heavens her father was a big man like Jackson. The ring was a tight fit, but it would work. "With this ring, I thee wed, and pledge my life, my love and my honor, committing my heart and my soul to you and you alone from this day forward."

Bridger stared down at it, then up at her and broke into a broad smile.

He didn't wait for permission to kiss her. He yanked

her into his body and proceeded to kiss the socks off her.

Laughter and applause rolled out.

When at last they came up for air, she looked into the eyes she loved so much. "Thank you for not giving up on me. For not letting me be an idiot."

His mouth quirked. "My pleasure, Legs." Then he drew her hands to his lips and kissed each one. "Thank you for giving me a home in your heart, in your town, in your life. We're going to make a good life here."

"We are."

"Well, I think that says it all, folks. May I present to you Mr. and Mrs. Bridger Calhoun?"

Ruby's house filled with loud applause and shouts.

Then a little voice pierced the din.

"Bwidge, are we married now?"

She never saw Bridger at a loss for words—

But he was in that state now, a panicked expression on his face as he sought out Maddie and Boone.

Lilah Rose's father pulled her close to explain the situation.

While Penny dropped her head and laughed until her sides ached.

Then found herself swept off her feet.

"Laugh it up, Shark Girl."

But Bridger was smiling like the sun.

"That's Mrs. Shark Girl to you, mister."

She didn't wait for Bridger to answer.

Instead it was he who was thoroughly kissed.

~THE END~

Thank you for letting me share my stories with you!

If you enjoyed TEXAS CHRISTMAS BRIDE, I would be very grateful if you would help others find this book by recommending it to your friends in such places as GOODREADS, BOOKBUB and writing a review. If you would like to be informed when my next release is available, please sign up for my newsletter by visiting my website at www.jeanbrashear.com and follow me on BookBub.

Next up is THE BOOK BABES:

The Book Babes reading group began as five women wanting to talk books—but now they've become family. There's romance author Ava Sinclair, organizer and backbone; happily-married mother of five Ellie Preston, group mom; patrician art gallery owner Sylvie Everett; single mom and sociology professor Luisa Martinez; and ambitious attorney Laken Foster, the wild child of the bunch. For several years now, they've met monthly and discussed the current book a little—and dissected their lives and loves far more often.

But now change is rippling through the group, begun by Laken's restlessness with her freewheeling life of serial hookups and sent into hyperdrive by Ava's suddenly-hot career, while Luisa's abusive ex tries to reclaim their teenage son and Sylvie faces her mother's decline. But it's when Ellie takes her first step into life after her children fly the nest and falls under the spell of the sexy artist who's teaching her to paint that the group's orbit begins to wobble on its axis, and life—for all of them and the men they love—will never be the same.

And then there's the surprise Sweetgrass Springs connection…

Start reading THE BOOK BABES today!

I love hearing from you, so please contact me through any of the options at the end of this book.

Thanks!
Jean

Please enjoy an excerpt from THE BOOK BABES:

"You answered a freaking personals ad?" Ava Sinclair burst out laughing. "Which one, Laken? *Six foot tall hunk of burning love seeks woman into foot massage and Bob Marley?*"

Three other heads swiveled, waiting for the inevitable flare-up when Ava's exasperation overcame her love, and Laken Foster's shark-lawyer ego couldn't stand coming in second.

"Laken, you didn't," Luisa Martinez protested, her soft voice barely heard above the sudden din. She squeezed Laken's hand in commiseration.

Laken shot her a look that forbade pity. Luisa settled back to drink her tea and wait.

"Well, I for one, darling, think it's about time you made the switch from the singles bar scene. All those dreadful married men with white bands on their fingers." Sylvie Everett's elegant nose wrinkled faintly. "Now tell all. Dish the details. What's he like? Any orgies in the offing?"

Ava watched as Ellie Preston returned to her cozy living room, fresh wine bottles in hand. Ava could have predicted the rescue.

She wasn't wrong. Ellie eased in between them,

soothing. "Now, Sylvie. Laken may not want to talk about it. More wine, anyone?"

"Since when does Laken withhold a single detail of her sex life?" Ava couldn't resist prodding Ellie's perpetual air of virginity. The mother of five, her baby about to start first grade, Ellie could pass for sixteen in all but the harshest light. There was something of the ingénue about their auburn-haired friend that life couldn't seem to erase. The room around them reflected her: lush green plants at every window, the bright spill of knitting yarns in a basket, pillow tops she'd quilted by hand.

The dusting of freckles across Ellie's nose dimmed as her cheeks turned pink. Then her grin turned impish. "Well, far be it from me to discourage her from talking about it—" Her eyebrows rose with her voice. "—if she wants to?"

The whole group broke up laughing, Laken's sultry chuckles blending with Luisa's clear soprano.

"Come on, Laken, spill your guts. Luisa hasn't been laid in two years and Ellie's still trying to figure out where all those kids come from." Ava poured herself a second glass of pinot noir.

Laken slugged down the last of her wine, holding out the glass for Ellie to refill. Her spiky dark mane shook with the force of her denial. "You do not have my permission to steal this for your next book, Ava."

Ava clutched one hand to her breast with a dramatic sigh. "Trust me, Laken, I haven't run out of imagination yet. This crew has a ways to go to catch up with my heroines."

"Too true," Sylvie nodded. "Thanks to your incredible imaginary men." She lifted her glass. "To Ava's heroes, long may they inspire our dreams."

They all clicked glasses, laughing, and drank—Luisa her tea, Ellie her watered wine, Ava and Laken red, Sylvie her customary chardonnay.

Another meeting of The Book Babes was well underway.

Laken sprawled back and sighed, fanning herself against the summer swelter of Austin, Texas. "If only you could conjure some of them up in the flesh, Ava, I wouldn't be reduced to scouring the earth for one good man."

"There are good men all around you," Ellie objected.

"Yeah, but you and Ava are married to them."

"Wyatt has a friend—"

"Stop right there," Laken flashed her palm at Ellie. "No more matchmaking. Period. There are three men in this town worth a damn; Ava's got Tom, you've got Wyatt, and Sylvie's going to keep Gabe waiting until he's old and gray."

"No, Sylvie's not." A tiny tremor shook the carefully modulated voice that matched Sylvie's ever-faultless appearance.

Ava shot a glance across the coffee table, seeing what she should have recognized earlier in Sylvie's silence. "What happened?"

Sylvie shook her head, the ash blonde shoulder-length pageboy shimmering. "It's over, that's all."

Ever the nurturer, Ellie placed a hand on Sylvie's shoulder. Only Ellie would dare, and only Ellie would not be shaken off by shoulders tightened into almost military posture. "You don't have to talk about it, if you don't want to."

"I don't."

Silence stretched out, an unheard-of occurrence at their monthly meetings. Far more common was the clamor of all of them talking at once, too much to say, too much to share, words tumbling in pell-mell fashion from the lips of intelligent women trying to piece out the ways of the world.

Luisa filled in with their topic of last resort—the book they were supposed to be discussing. "So what did anyone think of *Smilla's Sense of Snow*?"

Ava held back. She'd hated its dearth of emotion. The plot was intriguing, but the writing was so spare and sterile. But she knew that Sylvie had loved it, and Sylvie was already hurting.

Laken had no such restraint. "It sucked."

"Laken!" Ellie reached over, patting Sylvie's knee. "It was really interesting. Very exciting."

"I loved it, Sylvie," Luisa responded. "I had to wrap up in a blanket, reading it, the setting was so vivid."

Ava chuckled and shook her head. A blanket in August in Texas. "What was the a/c setting? Fifty-five?"

Laken intoned, "Thank God summer doesn't last forever."

Sylvie's smooth tones interrupted their laughter. "What about you, Ava? How did you like it?"

Opening her mouth to respond, Ava glanced around the room, distracted by the tears brimming on Ellie's lashes. Ava's comments were forgotten as she took in the startling sight. "What's wrong, Ellie?"

The auburn pageboy swung with the shaking of Ellie's head, her fingers pressed tightly to trembling lips.

Even the Ice Queen was disturbed by the sight. Ellie always smiled, always ministered to the rest of them. "Is it one of the children?" Sylvie ventured.

The tears overflowed ginger lashes, brown eyes filled with hurt. "I swore I wouldn't do this. It's silly…millions of women deal with this. I know it's dumb, but—" She shook her head again, dropping her gaze. "Sam's starting first grade, and Christy is leaving for college, and all of a sudden, all I can think is: what happens when they're all gone?"

Ava and Luisa exchanged glances. The empty nest. It hit everyone. Laken and Sylvie had no children; they could look sympathetic, but they'd never truly understand.

She tried for reason. "It's a long time until Sam leaves the nest, kiddo."

Ellie sniffed. "I know that. Intellectually, I understand all of this. But it doesn't change the fact that being a mother is all I know how to be. Look at you, Ava. You've created a whole new life, becoming a writer. You're excited and alive and—"

"—crazed and despairing and insane to have tried it."

Ellie brushed at her eyes. "But the fact remains that you know what you're doing with your life. You're a mother, but you're not only a mother. Luisa has her Ph.D. and tenure—"

"And a mother driving me nuts."

Ellie ignored her, leaning forward. "Laken's a successful lawyer, Sylvie's got her gallery. What do I do that's interesting? I drive carpools and bake cupcakes and do laundry and feed the damn chickens." For Ellie to swear was almost earth-shattering.

"And lead Scouts and sew and garden—hell, Ellie, you can do anything," Laken's voice rose above the others.

"Jack of all trades, master of none."

Ava drew a breath to respond, but Sylvie beat her to it.

"You need to be painting, Ellie. It's criminal that you ignore your talent."

Ellie blushed. "I just fool around. I've never had lessons."

"Anyone can take lessons. You have a gift."

Ava could see that Sylvie meant it. Sylvie's life revolved around art; it was the great sorrow of her life to have an unerring eye for the beautiful, for startling new talent—and to be unable to draw with more than mediocrity herself. Sylvie did not suffer fools gladly; even with her great affection for Ellie, an alliance that surprised them all, she would never say something she didn't mean. Saving feelings was never a priority with Sylvie.

Ava added her weight to the proposition. "I only had two children, not your five, but I know all too well the toll a family takes. You need to be feeding your soul, Ellie. You've still got a long way to go down this road of life, and you have a right to reserve some of it for yourself. You give everything to Wyatt and the kids, but Wyatt is a grown man, and the kids will need you less and less as they get older. It's time to start thinking about Ellie."

"But I know how fast it goes. Before I know it, Sam will be leaving for college. I can't miss these years."

"Come on, Ellie," Laken's dry tones crackled. "You're not talking about abandoning them. You can do this while they're all at school."

"But they're not used to—"

Ava spoke gently. "Your kids are great and amazingly unspoiled, but they won't die if you don't lie down in the road to be run over by them."

Ellie blew her nose, her back stiffening. "I don't do that."

Luisa's hand touched her gently. "What Ava means is that you give yourself to everyone you know, including us, and never reserve anything for yourself. We're all very lucky that you do, *chica*, but you have to look out for yourself, too."

"The well runs dry, kiddo," Ava reasoned. "Nothing faster than a family to drain you. Cut yourself some slack and think of it this way: if you're happier, they'll be happier."

"I should be happy now."

Ava waved a dismissive hand. "We should all be happy. None of us are starving in Africa, we all have roofs over our heads, we have love in our lives—"

"Speak for yourself," Laken said dryly.

Ava shot her a glare. "All right, everyone but Laken has love in her life, but constant hot sex is a workable substitute—"

The entire group broke up laughing. Even Ellie

grinned.

…Excerpt from THE BOOK BABES *by Jean Brashear ©
2015*

Start reading THE BOOK BABES today!

THE SWEETGRASS SPRINGS Series in order:

TEXAS ROOTS (Ian and Scarlett)

TEXAS WILD (Mackey and Rissa)

TEXAS DREAMS (a reunion of all the Texas Heroes
families)

TEXAS REBEL (Jackson and Veronica)

TEXAS BLAZE (Bridger and Penelope)

TEXAS CHRISTMAS BRIDE (a Texas Heroes reunion)

THE BOOK BABES (introducing Michael and Laken)

TEXAS HOPE (Michael and Laken)

TEXAS STRONG (Tank and Chrissy)

TEXAS SWEET (Brenda and Henry)

BE MINE THIS CHRISTMAS (Gib and Dulcie)

TEXAS CHARM (Jeanette and Walker)

TEXAS MAGIC (Dominic and Lexie)

BE MY MIDNIGHT KISS (Steph and Gavin)

BOOKS BY JEAN BRASHEAR:

SWEETGRASS SPRINGS

Nestled in the Texas Hill Country, tiny Sweetgrass
Springs was founded by four veterans of the Texas
Revolution, and for over a century the town and their

ranches grew and prospered. Nowadays, however, too many of the town's children leave for the big city as soon as they can escape, and Sweetgrass is barely hanging on. The heart and soul of Sweetgrass is Ruby Gallagher. Her daughter vanished from Sweetgrass right after high school, but Ruby, owner of community gathering place Ruby's Café, remains, keeping vigil, hoping for her daughter's return. She is fighting to save her ancestors' legacy, but the town is dying, and it's breaking Ruby's heart.

Then the granddaughter she never knew existed arrives and sets in motion a new life for this eccentric, lovable spot in the road…where hope never fades and love never dies. Readers call it "a special place for hearts that need healing."

Texas Roots: A Paris-trained chef on the run finds Texas family she never knew existed and a sexy cowboy she doesn't dare love

Texas Wild: Sexy SEAL turned Hollywood stuntman returns home to find his buddy's little sister all grown up

Texas Dreams: Take two reluctant brides and two frustrated grooms, mix with both clans of Gallaghers and season with a SEAL or three, a movie star, a Hollywood Barbie and a country music giant—and get not one but two surprise weddings

Texas Rebel: A former rebellious teen turned billionaire's reunion with his teenage sweetheart and a secret baby he never knew about

Texas Blaze: What happens when a shark lawyer in stilettos has a fling with a hot firefighter determined to find Suzy Homemaker?

Texas Christmas Bride: All he wants is the girl he thought he'd lost forever.

The Book Babes: Five women began as a reading group and became family...but now change is rippling through the group.

Texas Hope: Can two brothers who never knew each other existed overcome the secrets of a woman who abandoned one son and lied to the other?

Texas Strong: Can a man who's never trusted anyone and a woman who's trusted all the wrong men defy the odds and open their hearts to each other?

Texas Sweet: When a stranger who holds the keys to her identity arrives in town, will the girl everyone knows as Brenda come to terms with her past or run again?

Be Mine This Christmas: The man he's become is not the boy she once knew—and he may never forgive her, once he knows the secret she's been concealing.

Texas Charm: He's a country superstar; she's a small town waitress. When the real world slams into their reverie, whose heart will be the one to break? (Contains an original song written for this book)

Texas Magic: One billionaire…one tomboy…one night of magic. Miracle or mirage?

Be My Midnight Kiss: It's New Year's Eve…and now or never for these two hearts

Boxed sets:

The Gallaghers Of Sweetgrass Springs Boxed Set 1 (Books 1-3)

The Gallaghers Of Sweetgrass Springs Boxed Set 2 (Books 4-6)

Finding Home Boxed Set One (Sweetgrass Springs Stories)

Finding Home Boxed Set Two (Sweetgrass Springs Stories)

THE GALLAGHERS OF MORNING STAR
(cousins of the Sweetgrass Springs clan)

Secrets will be revealed and the lives of four people will be shattered as they learn that who they are and where they come from is not at all what they always believed.

Texas Secrets: Former SEAL Boone Gallagher returns to the only home he's ever known only to find that the ranch has been willed to a stranger who doesn't want it—and he must keep her there for thirty days, or it will be lost to them both.

Texas Lonely: A loner who's lost faith in love is the only hope for a mother and child on the run

Texas Bad Boy: Disgraced bad boy has his chance for revenge against the beautiful society girl who chose money over his love

The Gallaghers Of Morning Star Boxed Set

LONE STAR LOVERS

Heart-tugging, action-packed and passionate stories of the close-knit Sullivan/Sandoval family of four brothers and one sister, plus the three Morgan sisters, orphaned and separated for many years, whose lives reconnect as they become part of the family circle.

Texas Heartthrob: Hollywood's hottest star is a man in disguise when he encounters a woman who's lost everything...but her secrets. When the world catches up to them, will the price of their lies cost them everything?

Texas Healer: Special Forces medic holds the power to heal both a doctor's injured body and her wounded heart...but she can't stay in his world—and he can't leave.

Texas Protector: A detective forever haunted by the night when he couldn't save a young girl from trauma—now she's a cop herself and he has to send her undercover to lure a murderer.

Texas Deception: A plucky crusader falls for a down-on-his-luck stranger—only to learn too late that he's the villain determined to destroy her town

Texas Lost: A hard-nosed detective targeted by internal affairs and the woman who's professional evaluation will make or break his career. A a growing attraction between them risks first his case…and then her life.

Texas Wanderer: When she's lost all her dreams and is finally finding a place to call home, will she place her trust—and her heart—in the hands of a wanderer with secrets?

Texas Bodyguard: He's undercover as a bodyguard to a film star because her best friend is his top suspect. When she comes to mean too much to him, confessing his deception means risking his career—but not coming clean with her could risk her life

Texas Rescue: A haunted warrior who lives in the shadows encounters a small, valiant woman who's a champion of lost causes, and the vibrant light within her lures him from the darkness. When she is rocked by a brush with evil, can he make her feel safe again…and can she convince him that he deserves to live in the light?

Lone Star Lovers Boxed Set (Books 1-3)

THE MARSHALLS

Texas Refuge: Haunted former detective is the only sanctuary for an actress being stalked by a madman

Texas Star: Sexiest Man Alive becomes a white knight for a woman who keeps trying to escape him

Texas Danger: Down on his luck rancher is the only hope for a socialite on the run from the mob

The Marshalls Boxed Set

SECOND CHANCES series

Love deserves a second chance…

Guarding Gaby: Gabriela Navarro believed she and Eli Wolverton would always be together…until he abandoned her.

Bringing Bella Back: They had the perfect marriage…until he lost his way. Then he lost Bella.

The Price He Paid: The golden boy and the rebel girl who cost him everything

The House That Love Built: Once they had it all: a home with a man who adored her, three children they cherished, a life filled with passion and promise. Until one troubled child cost them everything.

The Road Back Home: Can her family forgive what she can't forgive herself?

Dream House: Her dream house is the scene of his nightmares.

THE GODDESS OF FRIED OKRA

"Wholly original, funny and poignant"

~#1 New York Times bestselling author Susan Wiggs

Every life has signposts.
Every traveler has a history.
Sometimes a detour is the only way home

Lost and grieving, Eudora "Pea" O'Brien sets off on a road trip to find her sister, collecting an unlikely family of strays along the way to discovering where she truly belongs.

DANGEROUS TO LOVE stories

Is he her enemy…or will he save her?

Dark, deadly and dangerous, they operate in the shadows, guarding the women they love but cannot have.

The Choice: Only one of them can win—and if they cannot learn to trust each other, both of them could die.

Mercy: He went to prison for twenty years to save her…can he save her again?

The Light Walker: A brand-new detective. A mesmerizing, mysterious billionaire suspect. A powerful attraction that threatens the balance in a battle between the dark and the light

Dangerous To Love Boxed Set

Cookie Day Recipes

Note: The lovely ladies with whom I quilt weekly kindly contributed these cookie recipes for your own Cookie Day

Double Chocolate Oatmeal Cookies
Joyce Walden
Favorite quilt pattern: anything with cats

1 ½ cups sugar

1 cup margarine, softened

1 egg

¼ cup water

1 tsp. vanilla

1 ¼ cups flour

1/3 cup cocoa

½ tsp. baking soda

½ tsp. salt

3 cups quick-cooking oats

12-oz pkg. semi-sweet chocolate chips

Mix sugar, oleo, egg, water and vanilla. Stir in remaining ingredients.

Drop dough by rounded teaspoonful about 2 inches apart onto ungreased cookie sheet.

Bake at 350 degrees until almost no indentation remains, 10-12 minutes.

Remove immediately from cookie sheet.

Makes approximately 3 dozen cookies.

Chocolate Chip Cookies
Mel Brown
Favorite Quilt Pattern: Nine Patch

2 ½ cups flour

1 tsp. baking soda

1 tsp. salt

1 cup shortening

1 cup sugar

½ cup brown sugar

2 eggs

2 tsp. vanilla

Semi-sweet chocolate chips to taste

Chopped pecans to taste

Measure flour, soda and salt.

Cream shortening, add sugars, eggs and vanilla. Mix well.

Add flour mixture, chips and pecans.

Drop on ungreased cookie sheet about 2 inches apart.

Bake 375 degrees 10-12 minutes.

Makes 3-4 dozen cookies.

Cowboy Cookies
Ruth Sudduth
Favorite Quilt Pattern: Scrap Happy

3 cups flour

3 tsp. baking powder

3 tsp. baking soda

3 tsp. cinnamon

1 tsp. salt

3 sticks butter at room temperature

1 ½ cups white sugar

1 ½ cups brown sugar

3 large eggs, beaten

3 tsps. vanilla extract

3 cups semi-sweet chocolate chips

3 cups old fashioned rolled oats

2 cups sweetened flaked or shredded coconut

2 cups chopped pecans

Preheat oven to 350 degrees with racks in upper and lower third. Line two large baking sheets with parchment paper.

In a large bowl, vigorously whisk together the flour, baking powder, baking soda, cinnamon and salt.

Place butter in a standing electric mixer and beat on medium speed until smooth and light, about 1 minute. Slowly add in the white sugar and brown sugar, and beat to combine, about 2 more minutes. Add half the eggs, beat, then add the other half and beat again. Add the vanilla extract and beat again.

Lower the speed of the mixer to low and slowly add the flour mixture until just combined. Add the chocolate chips, oats, coconut and pecans, mixing until just combined.

If you like chewy cookies, drop about ¼ cup lumps of the dough onto the prepared cookie sheets, separated by 3 inches to allow for enough room for the cookies to spread as they cook. Bake for 7-9 minutes, then rotate the cookie sheets front to back and top to bottom, then bake for an additional 7-9 minutes. Cook them until the edges are browned, but not the whole cookie.

For crisper cookies, use about 2 Tbsp. of dough per cookie and cook for 13-16 minutes, rotating half way. Cook them until they are all nicely browned.

Remove from oven and let cool on the baking sheets for 5 minutes. Then remove the cookies to a rack to cool completely.

Makes 4-6 dozen cookies.

Gingersnaps
Linda Vise
Favorite Quilt Pattern: Bow Tie

1 cup shortening

2 ¼ cups sugar (reserve ¼ cup for dipping cookies before baking)

2 eggs

½ cup molasses or white Karo syrup

4 cups flour

2 tsp. baking soda

2 tsp. cinnamon

2 tsp. ground cloves

2 tsp. ground ginger

Sift together flour, baking soda, cinnamon, cloves and ginger.

Cream shortening with sugar; beat in eggs. Add molasses or Karo and mix in.

Add in dry mixture and mix.

Roll into 1 inch balls; dip the top of each in sugar.

Place on greased baking sheet 2 inches apart.

Bake at 375 degrees 15-18 minutes.

Makes 5 dozen cookies

English Breakfast Scones
Ceci Sinnwell
Favorite Quilt Pattern: Wedding Ring

In large bowl blend:
1 cup softened butter
2 ½ cup sugar
4 eggs
2 tsp. vanilla
2 tsp. cinnamon
¼ cup buttermilk
6 oz. dried cranberries
1/2 box golden raisins

Add:
5 cups flour
1 teas. baking powder
1 teas. baking soda

Preheat oven to 350 degrees, spray a nonstick pan (i use pampered chef)

Use a tablespoon to drop batter into cookie sheet.

Bake until scones are slightly browned and firm to the touch.

After done drizzle with frosting.

Frosting:
Blend 21/2 cup powdered sugar
1 teas. vanilla
add buttermilk to liquefy (1/4 cup or more)
until mixture runs off spoon.

Lemon Squares
Earlene Dorsa
Favorite Quilt Pattern: Log Cabin

2 cups flour

1 cup butter, softened

½ cup confectioner's sugar

Combine flour, butter and powdered sugar. Pat into two ungreased 8-inch square pans. Bake at 350 degrees for 20 minutes.

Filling:

4 eggs

2 cups sugar

4 Tbsp. flour

1 tsp. baking powder

4 Tbsp. lemon juice

2 tsp. grated lemon peel

Additional confectioner's sugar for dusting

For filling, in a second bowl, beat eggs. Add sugar, flour, baking powder, lemon juice and peel; beat until froths. Pour over crust. Bake 25 minutes longer or until golden.

Cool on wire rack. Dust with powdered sugar. Cut into bars.

Makes 18 bars

Nutritious Cookies
Jane Shurtleff
Favorite Quilt Pattern: Grandmother's Flower Garden

Cream together:
1 cup shortening
2/3 cup sugar
2/3 cup brown sugar

Add:
2 eggs
1 tsp. vanilla
Mix well

Sift together:
2 cups flour
2 tsp. baking soda
2 tsp. baking powder
Gradually add to cream mixture

Add to mix one at a time:
2 cups corn flakes
2 cups oatmeal
1 cup coconut (3.5 oz. can is 1 cup)
1 ½ cup chopped pecans

You may have to mix this by hand. Drop on greased cookie sheet 2 heaping Tbsp. at a time. Mold by hand if necessary

Bake 350 degrees 8 minutes only.

Makes 5-5 ½ dozen.

Bar Cookies
Linda Johnson
Favorite Quilt Pattern: Tumbling Blocks

1 stick butter, melted in 13x9 pan

1 cup graham cracker crumbs, sprinkled over butter

1 small package (approx. 12 oz.) chocolate chips

1 small package (approx. 12 oz.) butterscotch chips

1 cup coconut

1 cup chopped nuts, your preference

1 can sweetened condensed milk

Layer chocolate chips, butterscotch chips, coconut and nuts over butter/graham cracker mixture. Pour sweetened condensed milk over top. Press lightly.

Bake 350 degrees 30 minutes.

Cut into small bars, approximately 2 inches square. Makes about 2 dozen

Jackson's Sand Tarts
Jean Brashear
Favorite Quilt Pattern: Dresden Plate

2 cups butter at room temperature (do not substitute)
¾ cup sifted confectioner's sugar
4 cups sifted flour
1 Tbsp. cold water
1 ½ tsp. vanilla
2 cups chopped pecans
Additional sifted confectioner's sugar

Cream butter and sugar; add flour and water and blend well.

Stir in vanilla and pecans.

Roll into small balls (teaspoon-size) and place on ungreased cookie sheets.

Bake at 325 degrees for 5-8 minutes or until golden.

Roll in confectioner's sugar while still warm.

Makes 12 dozen. Will freeze well.

* * *

About the Author

A letter to Rod Stewart resulting in a Cinderella 16th birthday for her daughter might have been the first step on Texas romance author Jean Brashear's path to being a *New York Times* and *USAToday* bestselling author of more than 50 novels in romance and women's fiction.

Jean's stories are hailed as "feel-good romance at its finest" and her quirky small towns are called "a special place for hearts that need healing." All are evidence of Jean's heartfelt belief that love is the most powerful force in the universe, and her stories reflect that bone-deep commitment to spreading her faith in the goodness that exists inside us all.

Connect With Jean

Visit Jean's website: www.jeanbrashear.com

Facebook: www.facebook.com/AuthorJeanBrashear

BookBub: www.bookbub.com/authors/jean-brashear

Pinterest: www.pinterest.com/JeanBrashear

Instagram: www.instagram.com/jeanbrashear

To be notified of new releases and special deals, sign up for Jean's newsletter on her website

Made in the USA
Monee, IL
08 May 2023

33338729R00132